THOSE

WHO
LONG

W.G. TUTTLE

THOSE WHO LONG

A NOVEL

THIS IS A
W.G. TUTTLE
BLURRED INK, LLC BOOK PRODUCTION

Riveting fiction.

Novels

Those Who Long
Try To Sleep
October Midnight
War For The Spheres

Short Stories

Adamah - A Book of the Serpent
Scranton October 1894
SURvIVe
Cut-Up
Where Did THEY Come From?
Standard Issue Spirits
Vacation's End
A Fatal Thing

For my wife Shawn

1

LIGHT shined through curtain-less windows into the bedroom. The day had started without Thad E. Hadet, who still laid in bed. Days come and go, as do nights, and they come and go whether people keep time with them or not. Some would say this personal disregard seems cruel. That no one really matters.

And that would be true. Not to the Earth. A harsh reminder that the world revolves around the Sun and no particular person. Never had. Never will.

Thad knew the world does what it had always done. And keeping time was not included. Man came up with years, months, days, hours, minutes, and seconds in an attempt to follow along. No one is bigger than the world.

So, through Thad E. Hadet's mere forty-two years, two months, six days, eight hours, twenty-five minutes, and seven seconds and counting, he occupied space in the shadows, waiting.

Outside of being in a coma, no one alive could sleep forever. The body rested for so long, then had to get going again. Call it life's force or whatever you want, but it happens that way for all of us.

Dying in his sleep wasn't in the cards for Thad. Not this time, anyway. Maybe one of these nights. Or mornings. Or while taking a nap. Just maybe. There was always a chance. And, no matter how big or small, chance enticed people into taking them.

Thad rocked once on his side, scratched his nose, then a buttcheek. Opposite of many people, his flesh was willing, but his spirit was weak. He didn't want to get up and face the day, anything, or anyone. But his mind and body forced him awake. One or both contained the lifeforce, not Thad's will.

Sure, swallowing a few sleeping pills would do the trick, but not permanently, unless he overdosed on them. But Thad didn't believe in suicide. Hell, he didn't even believe in taking sleeping pills. If the mind and body weren't ready to sleep, then he would just have to wait until they were. When they wanted to wake up, let them. Who was he to say otherwise?

All he could do was rest or rise with them. For Thad's *true self*, whether in his mind or someplace in the body like the heart, didn't have a choice. Either way, his *true self* was contained in the body. Without the body, it's debatable whether life exists, for the body is evidence of life.

Everyone's lifeforce has its own timing. Thad understood that, too. It ran until it ceased. Much in the same way as the Earth. Unless, of course, someone or something abruptly ended it. To say acts carried out in this fashion weren't known by the lifeforce may contain an arrogant ignorance. No one knows where this force comes from, let alone how much or little it knows.

Thad turned onto his back and opened his

eyes. Instead of trying to figure out what wasn't and would never be understood, he simply waited. People he had come across over the years who had pursued such endeavors found only confusion and frustration, rather than answers and enlightenment, so why bother.

The sun's warmth kissed his cheeks in a gentle, empathetic way, which warmed his insides, too. A feeling of affirmation that the sun itself seemed to agree that waiting was right, acceptable, how every living thing should exist. Striving and wrestling only lead to struggle and difficulty. Why bother. So, Thad didn't.

Thad closed his eyes and crossed his arms over his chest. He imagined what it might be like when the waiting was over.

And failed miserably. Imaginations can run buck-naked, free, and wild, but no one knows for sure what lies beyond *the waiting*.

He pulled the sheet up over his head loosely, closed his eyes, and crossed his arms over his chest to see if it would help. It didn't. It never did. Every time he imagined himself lying in a casket with the lid closed, it occurred to him that, when that day came, he would be dead. And no one knows what death is. Not really. So, trying to imagine something beyond imagining—beyond *the waiting*—seemed futile.

But Thad did anyway. A lot. In this way, he wasn't any different than those *other* people, who searched for answers, because he was searching for answers, too. And, as what happens in searching, people tend to trample over the same old ground. Mentally being where they had already been, they never get anywhere, especially when it comes to death.

Thad wasn't exempt. Every morning since the age of twelve, this exercise of pulling the sheet up over his head, closing his eyes, crossing his arms over his chest, and imagining lying in a coffin happened religiously. Grass will never grow again on this beaten-down path. Nor should it. Especially when this searching entailed familiarizing himself with death for the sake of death and had nothing to do with enriching his life or spawning a sense of gratitude for each new day.

Will I imagine? Thad whispered, his breath raising the sheet slightly above his mouth. *Will I dream?*

2

THAD'S mind and body were right in getting Thad out of bed. Thad knew it, too. His mind made sure he knew it. There was something vitally important he needed to do today. It was as if the lifeforce driving his mind and body knew what needed to be done and allowed Thad to complete it before something happened to him and it dropped into the unfinished business bucket as happens when people never get around to things before passing.

After shaving, brushing his teeth, and showering, Thad, with only a towel wrapped around his pelvis, reached to the very back of his hanging-closet and pulled out clothes on a hanger, wrapped in a plastic dry-cleaning bag. A three-piece suit—what he was to be buried in when the time came.

Dressed and ready, he checked himself in the mirror and agreed that nothing beat a basic black suit when it came to funerals. Black goes with everything, it's true, even with any coffin color.

And mood. One should always cater to the mood. A somber atmosphere must always have black incorporated into it. Gray was an elegant alternative. The darker, the better. Dismal. Otherwise, the ambiance would be all wrong. Always, the ambiance of a funeral should capture the loss. A dark day, indeed.

Dressed and ready for the day, Thad checked himself in the mirror. Damn, the black suit looked sharp on him. A perfect fit and look. What a great choice. What a great buy.

Pleased with how he looked in the mirror, Thad imagined himself at his own funeral, lying in a classic gray coffin. Now, seeing it through the eyes of an attendee, boy did he look, well—like he was sleeping—as he should.

Together, the corpse and its storage capsule were always the focal points of any traditional service and, in this case, would certainly set the mood. What a tragedy, yet, what a scene.

Thad couldn't get the image of himself lying in the coffin out of his mind. Picture perfect. About as picturesque as any funeral could be.

An anticipatory excitement filled him, wishing today was the day. If only he could see it. Who knows, maybe he will. If spirits exist, perhaps his might vacate the body and look down at the flesh and blood that had enprisoned it all of these years before departing for good.

Uh-oh. He was doing it again, being like those *other* people who overthink things.

So, he stopped. For now, anyway, knowing he would catch himself doing it again—like those *other* people. Until then, whatever will be, will be. Death could show up any time, any place, and in any way it wanted. All he could do was wait patiently.

Over his fixation with seeing himself lying in a coffin and having everything he needed for the day, Thad started for the door to his apartment.

A knock sounded outside.

Thad's lower jaw extended past his upper. He knew this would happen. Stuff like this made *waiting* so hard.

He looked through the peephole, saw who it was, cracked his neck, and opened the door.

"Yes, Mrs. Dray, may I help you?" Thad said.

Holding her cat and scratching it behind the ear with a finger, Mrs. Dray said, "Good morning, Thad. Just here to drop off little Muncie in your care."

A deep sigh carried away a few of Thad's breaths. The *wait* will be a few seconds shorter.

"Mrs. Dray," Thad said. "Didn't you read the paper I handed you yesterday when you picked up Muncie?"

"Paper?" she said. "I don't remember receiving a paper."

"You may not remember, Mrs. Dray, but I placed one in your hand."

"Well, I don't…"

"And what it said, Mrs. Dray, is that I won't be available today to watch Muncie or any of the other pets in the building because I'm going out."

"Well, what am I supposed to do with Muncie? I'm meeting friends for brunch then afternoon tea."

"I don't know, Mrs. Dray. I'm sorry. I'll watch Muncie tomorrow," Thad said, hoping tomorrow would never come and forced his way out of the apartment into the hall.

Reluctantly, Mrs. Dray retreated.

"Oh, my," she said. "I suppose I can see if Margaret is in, but then I'll have to make up something so she won't wonder why she wasn't invited to brunch and tea."

Locking his door, Thad said, "I'm sure you'll think of something, Mrs. Dray. Now, please excuse me, or else I'll be late."

3

THAD wasn't late. In fact, he had arrived a good half-an-hour early at the Will B. Still Funeral Home located at the edge of town. The building used to be a Masonic lodge until membership waned to twenty members, all of which integrated into a nearby lodge a town over, and the building went up for sale.

It remained on the market for a while. The biggest deterrent was the building itself, built with sandstone blocks each the size of an electric car—and no windows.

Yes, no windows. Not even on the door. Whatever these freemasons were doing, they didn't want any outsiders knowing about it.

Now, one freemason knew what had gone on in that windowless building and that was William Still. Yes, the owner of the Will B. Still Funeral Home located there now. Nearly forty years ago, the then twenty-eight-year-old Still had bought the lodge well below the original asking price, but a little above the lowest price to save face with the other freemasons who thought he was taking advantage of the brotherhood in buying a quality building cheap. Still was trying to do just that, but would never admit it. And he knew exactly what he was going to do with it—turn it into the best funeral home on this side of the state.

Now, thirty-nine years later and Mr. Still a ripening sixty-seven-years-old, his funeral home wasn't the best on this side of the state and never was. Not even the best in town. A fellow-freemason, Cecil Niwog, who also had participated in secrets behind those sandstone blocks, saw what William was trying to do and thought it was a good idea, so he bought the church at the other end of town, which was struggling with attendance and funding. Some modifications were required for the church building to handle everything a typical funeral home would, but since completion, the funeral home operation never failed an inspection.

Only known as the *Funeral Home*, per the generic sign out front, the building now serves as a place of worship for those long-time parishioners who had thought they had lost their church for good, as well as a funeral home. Unable to afford a pastor for some time, a few of the parishioners take turns leading services and Bible studies. Despite their best efforts, people have visited and left, with only one person, an eighty-year-old woman named Myrtle, staying.

This bummed-out the faithful, believing that the funeral home only strengthened their urgent message for unbelievers to accept God while they still could before they ended up lying in the funeral section and couldn't. Like Myrtle, who had worshiped with the congregation for five years before God had called her home and she had her turn to lie in the refrigerator on the other side of the building in the funeral section. Hard to believe that was three years ago.

Despite William Still's Funeral Home having the catchier name, which William had come up with himself, each home handled about half of the deaths that occurred in town.

It wasn't planned that way, how could it, nor did the owners agree to it, it just happened, mostly depending on who they know—or knew—and if the surviving family wanted windows during the viewing and service or not.

Now, no one could verify that the split between the funeral homes was even or not. It's not like anyone compared numbers. Sure, William and Cecil were trying to make a living, but neither wanted to be assholes about it. Preferences belonged to the families. And whatever funeral home they chose for whatever reason was up to them. William and Cecil shared information, but let the decisions to the families.

No deaths and no services scheduled for today, William walked through the door of the funeral home, carrying a coffee in one hand, a jelly donut in the other, and the morning paper tucked under his arm. An impatient bite of the donut speckled white powder all over his mouth.

Then he saw Gretchen, the cleaning lady, who William had hired on the cheap to come in anytime from close to open to clean up the place.

What a hire for William. No one could clean

like Gretchen. No one. Tiny but strong, she could clean rust out of metal. A young housewife in her thirties, she already knew all of the tricks of the trade—a seasoned domesticant. There wasn't anything she couldn't clean or disinfect.

And to think it all started when William stepped outside of the funeral home to smoke a cigar and saw Gretchen up on a ladder, cleaning decorative metal brackets of an awning on the house next door. William walked over and she must have already cleaned the one because it looked brand new, right off the shelf, instead of cleaned. The one she was working on started looking the same. Come to find out it was her house. It just so happened the housewife was looking to make a little extra money. William had said he could afford a little, so, after showing her what the job would entail, she took it.

Leave it to Cecil. He caught wind of William's new hire and paid Gretchen a visit, handing her a New Testament pocket Bible, compliments of the congregation. Cecil's pitch was short and sweet and ended with an offer of what he had hoped was more than what William was paying. It had been penciled on the inside cover of the tiny Bible.

It was more, and once Gretchen saw the

figure, she had one foot outside the Will B. Still Funeral Home.

That was until Cecil mentioned he wanted her to work particular hours.

So, with the Will B. Still funeral home next door and flexible hours, she stepped that foot right back inside and said she would think about it. Rather than declining the offer, she had kept it open-ended. That sent Cecil on his way with confidence.

A false confidence, because Gretchen had no intention of switching. Instead, she told Mr. Still of Mr. Niwog's offer and said she would go over there unless he paid more. William agreed and Gretchen had worked for him ever since.

"Hello," Mr. Still said to Gretchen, never getting out her name because some donut fell out of his mouth in enunciating the *o* in hello.

"Blasted!" he said, looking down at the mess on the floor.

"It's alright, Mr. Still," Gretchen said. "I'll get it before I leave."

A smile on her face like she knew something he didn't made him uncomfortable.

Mr. Still proceeded into the showroom and sat down at the conference table. The showroom was where he met with families to make arrangements or those seeking pre-planning. When no visitors were expected, he preferred it in there. It was much roomier than his office and had a larger window.

A few whole coffins, sections of caskets, urns, vases, flower arrangements, and several personalization examples crowded the edges and walls. *Convenient*, those in the business would say. *Practical*, realists would say. *Insensitive and pushy*, others would find this *death store*.

Mr. Still knew this, in coming across all-types. So, when he presented the options and pricing, he tried not to be an insensitive buttface about it. A few puffs on the old cigar and a swig, or two, or three of brandy beforehand usually relaxed him enough so he didn't come off like a jerkwad.

While Mr. Still sat at the conference table, chewing his last bite of donut, a sound came from behind the newspaper he was reading. He paused, took a sip of his coffee, then went back to reading.

The same sound occurred again.

Slowly, Mr. Still lowered the top of the paper below his eyes so he could see. Into the shadows of the showpieces at the other end of the room. He hadn't turned on the lights yet. Never did until nine a.m., opening time, or when it was too dark outside to read his newspaper with the light coming through the window.

One of the caskets shifted ever so slightly.

It happened, no question. Mr. Still didn't, for he saw it. It wasn't his eyes fooling him.

The same coffin shifted again.

Elevated on a stand made it easier to tell. If it were on the floor, it never would have moved. Watching, Mr. Still set the paper down on the conference table.

A crack appeared between the head and side panels. The casket was opening.

In the presentation room of the Will B. Still Funeral Home, the lid of the coffin slowly raised.

With his eyes fixed on the sight, William B. Still sat still in his chair.

The gap ever-widening, shadows danced inside the coffin. Until they weren't shadows any longer. Something black, solid, real, alive, moved inside. A tentacle appeared, pushing open the head-panel entirely, then retreating behind the darkness inside the box.

A black smear appeared just over the edge, then enlarged as the thing started to rise out of the coffin.

Wide-eyed on an otherwise expressionless face, Mr. Still watched.

The form took up much of the half-opened casket, now as tall as the raised lid.

Mr. Still licked his lips.

Its shadowed head seemed to turn, but it was hard to tell.

Staring, Mr. Still wet his lips again, tasting donut.

"Does this model come in gray?"

Mr. Still paused, took a sip of his coffee, and calmly said, "That particular model? I'll have to check. But I'm sure we can accommodate you with that or a similar one."

"It's comfortable," Thad said. "And new. This wasn't on your show-floor before."

"Just came in yesterday."

"Well, it's nice. I like it," Thad said, climbing out of the burial box.

Mr. Still stood. While retrieving a catalog off the shelf, he said, "Be careful. I'm not in the mood to be filing any claims."

"I will."

"Gretchen let you in?" Mr. Still slapped the catalog on the table.

"Yep."

Mr. Still nodded, thinking, *No wonder she was smiling this morning*, then he turned on the lights.

Thad stood by the coffin, running his hand over the silky-smooth material. It had felt pleasant around him inside, the plushness of the pillow under his head.

On his way back to the table, Mr. Still stopped and watched Thad caressing the coffin as if it was a woman's shapely, tanned leg on the beach. Waving a hand in Thad's direction, he sat down and flipped through the catalog.

Thad would have to check with Gretchen to make sure she was working her typical evenings this week. There was something he would like to do.

"Here it is," Mr. Still said. "It comes in gray. Actually, a few of them."

One last stroke of the eternal bedding—a bed made once and forever done—and Thad sat down across from Mr. Still.

Mr. Still situated the catalog so Thad could see.

"Let's see," he said. "They got Spanish-Gray, Cadet-Gray, Blue-Gray, Xanadu, Gunmetal, and Rocket Metallic."

Unsure, Thad said, "Well, I really wanted to stay with the classic gray I currently have."

"Look. Nobody's going to be studying the casket. Any examination of it usually comes down to whether it looks nice or not and that's it."

"You sure?"

"I'm sure. Think of it this way. A man's pink shirt is pink—that's it—no matter the shading. Only queers differentiate the shades by calling it salmon or some shit. And, hell, I know you aren't married, but I also know you aren't a—," he raised a bent wrist. "I've seen you checking out Gretchen in here. You should take the chance and go over there while her husband's at work and see if she'll let you enter her spa for an oil massage—if you catch my meaning."

"Yeah, but what if her husband finds out?"

Mr. Still leaned back in his seat and spread his hands. "You're all set, aren't you?"

Thad smiled. "I guess I am."

"Bet your ass," Mr. Still said, leaning forward in his seat. "There's not another person alive more prepared for death than you."

"*Gee*, thanks."

"I mean it. There's nothing more manly than a prepared man. Some prepare for a sporting event. Others war. You—death. And there's nothing wrong with that."

Thad cowered a bit. "Well, I dunno about that. Some find it weird…"

"Fuck 'em!" Mr. Still blurted. "Pre-planning your funeral is as smart as planning for any big event in life. I would argue, is there anything bigger than one's death? It's good for you. It's good for family and friends. And damn it, Thad, it's good for business."

"I know. You always supported me."

"*Damn straight!* As you do me. Now, what color is it going to be this week?"

"Whatever's closest to classic gray in that model."

Mr. Still leaned over the conference table. "You should open up a little bit, Thad. Expand your thinking. Consider other options. How about Gunmetal? *Jesus!*" He nearly knocked over his coffee. He looked around, then back at Thad. "Good thing we're not over at Cecil's funeral home *slash* church. The dead would rise and take holy vengeance on us both for taking the Lord's name in vain. Anyway, nothing's more hard-cocked than Gunmetal."

"I hear what you're preaching," Thad said. "But just gray."

Mr. Still laughed. "*Ah*, I see what you did there. Okay, okay. Basic gray."

"*Classic* gray."

"Pardon me, Mr.," Mr. Still raised a bent

wrist again, "—*classic* gray. To me, the Spanish-Gray looks damn close."

Mr. Still slid the catalog toward Thad for a better look.

Thad cleared his throat, then rolled his eyes down, capturing the color and texture of his suit. When he looked up, Mr. Still was staring at him.

Uncomfortable, Thad retreated to the catalog. Discretely, he positioned his arm on top of the catalog so his coat sleeve was beside the Spanish-Gray swatch. It was the best he could do, picturing himself in his classic black suit, lying in the Spanish-Gray casket. The scene enlivened with flowers, pictures, and guests.

Yes. It worked.

Waiting, Mr. Still sipped his coffee, not fooled by what Thad was doing. To him, who gave a fuck what color the casket was. No one will remember it, anyway. If he asked anyone what color the coffin was at the most recent funeral they intended, they wouldn't know. That's because the casket is only seen for a few hours. Besides that, half of it was usually opened for much of that time, so most people end up remembering the dead body. Between the handles for pallbearers, braces to hold them, other metal or wood on the outside of casket, and flowers—lots and lots of flowers—covering the death torpedo, there was barely any of the actual coffin left to see. The best chance was at the burial site when the lid was closed, but, even then, the flowers were put right back on and services there never last long, nor do people tend to stay, even family. Without question, services that entail lowering the casket into the ground was the absolute best time to see the casket for what it was before it disappeared into the grave and dirt thrown on top of the lid.

But, business was business. And Mr. Still liked Thad's visits, which gave the appearance of a bustling funeral home.

"Spanish-Gray, then," Thad said.

"In that model?" Mr. Still checked. He always checked. Until next week, when Thad would be stuck on another pre-planning detail before returning to the make, model, and color of the coffin.

"In that model," Thad verified. "And white material, same as before. What's the cost of that?"

"Let's see," Mr. Still said, looking it up and thinking, *Most people spend less time buying a car.* Mumblings to himself accompanied taps on a desk calculator, then he said, "About $3,500, give or take a hundred."

"That's five hundred more than where I was."

"I guess so. Maybe six. I don't remember."

"I do. It's five hundred over."

"You would know," Mr. Still said. "Let me see if Costa's in and what financial magic he can do to get that down some."

"Oh, all right," Thad agreed.

5

"COSTA'S not in, yet," Mr. Still announced, walking into the showroom after checking. "Do you want to wait? Maybe go over to Grethen's and see if her spa's open?"

"I'll wait," Thad said.

"Suit yourself. You know where the water fountain is."

Truth be told, Thad knew where everything was. And he never minded waiting. Not in the funeral home. The presentation room offered a lot. A little old-school, he preferred flipping through the catalogs rather than looking online.

He could spend hours doing that. Maybe it stemmed from childhood. Department store catalogs were how kids eyed what they wanted for Christmas or their birthday. A time before the personal computer and the Internet became commonplace in many American households. Without question, those inventions paired together saved a lot of trees.

But, what interested Thad more about the funeral home was the behind-the-scenes stuff that most people don't bother investigating while alive because they don't want to know. They'll learn it when they were dead. Which, of course, meant they wouldn't.

Thad wasn't so sure. Once more, that out-of-body spirit idea said, *Boo!* He was overthinking again—like *other* people.

"How about one of those tours?" Thad asked.

"Again?" Mr. Still scrunched his face. "Good God, man!"

"I get it. You're busy."

"That—and you've been given so many tours, I'm sure you could present it better than

anyone."

The two men looked at each other.

Mr. Still gave in. "I'll tell you what. How about you go on a self-guided tour this morning? I know that's what you would like to do, anyway."

"Really?"

Thad's excitement concerned Mr. Still.

"If," Mr. Still started. "And it's a big if. *If* you promise not to touch anything. I mean it. Nothing, Thad. Don't start the incinerator or take the hearse out for a drive or try the embalming fluid on yourself or any crazy shit like that. *Okay?* Promise me."

Giddy as a kid sitting on the floor in front of a bunch of presents nestled under a Christmas tree—*straight out of the department store catalog*—Thad promised.

"You ain't shitting me?"

"No, sir. I promise."

Although Thad was forty-two-years-old, like a child, he waited for William B. Still to dismiss him.

"I believe you," Mr. Still said. "But just in case you're planning on doing any harm to yourself, since you're here, dressed, and ready to go, know that it'll all be captured on video. And when the insurance company asks for those tapes, I'll have to give them to them. And you know what that means for your beneficiaries, don't you?"

"They won't get the money," Thad answered.

"That's right. I knew you would know that. *So*, if you were planning on screwing them out of their inheritance, it's none of my business. You already paid me—pending any incidentals, of course.

"What *is* my business is my funeral business. And the last thing I need is a suicide in here. Funeral homes already get a bad rap, let alone a rumor starts that you're haunting the place."

"Oh, I would never haunt your funeral home, Mr. Still," Thad assured.

"Damn right, you wouldn't! Because you're a straight shooter. But know if you did, I would chop your body into six hundred and sixty-six pieces, sear you in the incinerator, scatter you down on the beach, and let whatever comes along eat you. What would happen then if the resurrection was real?"

"Ressurection?"

The thought had never entered Thad's mind.

"You mean to tell me you never heard of the Christian resurrection in all of your years?" Mr. Still couldn't believe it. "Or any religion for that matter. In today's world of TV evangelists. Internet evangelists. Radio."

"Well, I…"

"Hell, I thought you remained around because of religious beliefs. If not that, *what?*"

"It's not that I'm against religion," Thad tried to explain. "Nor am I exactly for one either."

"I should be more surprised than I am. I've been on this Earth a long time and must say, I'm not sure what any religion's message is nowadays. And if *I* don't know, something tells me *they* don't either. I mean, how hard could it be? But *I* know *my* message. And you must believe it. Are you a believer?"

"I just said I'm not for a particular religion," Thad answered.

"Not religion," Mr. Still said. "*My* message. About the funeral home."

"Well, you know I am."

"I do know you. Lord knows I can't say I don't. So, then go into all of the home, marveling in all that will someday be performed on you. Then leave here and don't bother stopping in to tell me goodbye. Show yourself out. And don't forget to tell others that the Will B. Still Funeral Home has a name, unlike that other funeral place across town. Ask them if a no-name funeral home is really what they want printed in their obituary, on their programs, and in their official records."

"Shouldn't I talk with Costa when he comes in?"

"Yes, but not me. We'll say our goodbyes for the day now. Do you understand?"

"Yes."

"Then go, and don't me see me until tomorrow."

As if addressing royalty, Thad bowed and said, "Thank you, Mr. Still."

6

OUTSIDE of the misunderstanding with Mrs. Dray this morning, this was shaping up to be a pretty good day. How good Thad looked in the suit he was to be buried in. Tweaking the casket so the service would be perfect. And now, an unexpected surprise: Mr. Still allowing him to tour the funeral home on his own.

He left the presence of Mr. Still with many questions, but the old man was clear that he did not want to see Thad again today and would see him at the earliest tomorrow.

Now—the tour.

It had been a while since Thad felt so free, cut-loose as it were. Although this could bring a sense of uncertainty with it, it didn't for Thad. In fact, the opposite. For there was no question where he would start or how he would proceed. Why change the tour just because he was on his own? The tour had always gone sequential. And sequential was how it was going to go when Thad's time came. Or went; however one looked at it.

Came for sure, as far as Thad was concerned. Because it all started when the hearse pulled into the funeral home garage with his body.

Thad trotted to the garage. He had only— *what?*—maybe six or seven hours if he skipped lunch before the funeral home closed. He would have checked his watch but didn't want to become depressed.

Ah, that's right. *Costa*. He would save that for another day. How many opportunities would he have like today? Basing on his relationship with Mr. Still, this may be it. Then again, as long as Thad didn't touch anything or do anything foolish, maybe, just maybe.

The garage didn't smell like a garage. In fairness, nothing had happened in there today. None of the vehicles had moved.

Thad walked over to the van, metallic gray, about the same color as his casket choice. The hood felt cool. Probably hadn't moved since hauling in Gus Gainell, who had died last week in his sleep.

In talking with Mr. Still, the story went Gus' daughter had paid her father, Mr. Gainell, a visit. With mail in hand, she found him lying in his recliner in the family room with the TV on. Thinking he was napping, she did some things around the house for him, including cleaning up the empty milk glass and TV dinner tray on the stand beside the chair. It wasn't until she started collapsing the stand that she realized he hadn't moved since she had arrived. His chest wasn't moving and she realized he wasn't breathing.

Yes, Mr. Still and other funeral home workers shared details like that with Thad, knowing two things. First, and the most important, Thad never shared such information with anyone else. Even with others associated with the funeral home. Second, Thad would buzz around them all day, driving everyone crazy. The only repellant that worked was divulging some information until he was satisfied and went away. Sometimes, that was the only way of dealing with him.

Thad wondered what it might be like dying while sleeping. *Did Death bother waking Mr. Gainell to at least let him know he was dying? Some kind of final pain, discomfort, or failure so he knew? Funny how Death sometimes didn't wake the person at their time of death. It just happens. The person slips from living to no longer living.*

Most believe dying in one's sleep is the way to go if you're lucky to get it. Peaceful. Maybe even blissful in ignorance of not knowing it's happening. Simply drifting from life into death without having to experience pain, some horrible confrontation or cause, and clueless.

But how does anyone know that to be true? Has anyone died in their sleep and come back to tell about it? Anyone claiming they had, are they crazy or telling the truth?

Thad found the whole idea of dying in his sleep unsettling. Because, to him, that's what it would be—unsettled. Unresolved. In the gray area. Did he die, or didn't he?

No, he would rather know when and how. A slower death would be welcomed for the sake of knowing those two things. Oh, yes, they would. Welcome, indeed. To Thad, *knowing* was peace.

Does Gus Gainell know he had died? Or is the poor

fellow trapped in a restless sleep? Fully expecting to wake up—but can't.

Thad caressed the hood of the van.

This brought Mr. Gainell in, he thought. *And Ms. Peachtree before him. Mr. Lockie before her.*

Thad could have named more from memory. Keeping track of the deaths in town was a duty of his. Don't ever say it was a hobby. Not to Thad. Names were logged as soon as he got the news. And although he did derive pleasure from making the entries, it still wasn't a hobby. No, the joy he felt could be described as a hopeful happiness for the departed. That something better awaited them on the other side. Not as strong as faith, but similar. Maybe, how it might feel logging names of Christians into the Book of Life.

Thad didn't know. Nor does anyone else. For him, it was more important never to forget those that had paved the way—the road to death.

Of course, death's road ended in a dead-end. It had to.

Who'd be next? Thad thought.

Him?

It was possible. People live their lives and drive until they run out of road. Reaching the end, it just ends—a dead end.

Of course, nowadays, medical science had

advanced to where, based on a diagnosed disease and status, it was possible to guesstimate how much road remained. But it wasn't an exact science yet. Perhaps, one day, parents will have a choice in knowing at birth how long their newborn(s) will live.

If the science was available now, Thad would like to know his approximate date of death. Then he would know whether the van he touched would be the vehicle to bring him in. Now, that all depended on the life of the van, as it were.

Will it still be in service? How about the other equipment? The funeral home?

Not so easy, this death stuff. Even for inanimate things like the van. No one knows for sure how the future will go. But Thad was doing his best to be prepared.

THAD moved to the back of the van, opened the back door, and scanned the garage. Not seeing anyone, he pulled the other door open and sat in the back of the vehicle. He leaned back on his elbows and took in the view. Before he knew it, he was on his back, lying on the rubber flooring. His feet dangled out, so he scooted himself back until he was entirely inside the van. As he had done in bed this morning, he crossed his arms comfortably over his chest and closed his eyes.

Gainell, Peachtree, Lockie, and others had all laid here—dead, Thad thought. *Brought to the funeral home.*

Whoever had cleaned the van had done a thorough job, for Thad couldn't smell—

Nope—wait a second—

There it was—the faint smell of death. Raw. Fleshy, yet earthy. Granular skin, which could be touched. And at the same time, nothingness, yet something was there. A lingering presence. *Them.* Lockie, Peachtree, and, most recently, Gainell.

But where did the smell come from? Thad didn't know. Maybe it was in the rubber. The metal. The air.

Highly unlikely. Carpet or fabric, sure. But not surfaces such as these. Not air that had been moved through and circulated.

So, from where?

Maybe one had to lay where they had lain. The dead. Something spiritual rather than scientific. A remnant. And Thad laid in it.

I'm probably the only living person to have laid in this van where only the deceased have, Thad thought, then after, *I hope I didn't contaminate it.*

That smell and lying where only the dead had lain, it didn't take long or much imagination before Thad sensed Billy in the driver's seat and Jimmy in the passenger's; two of Mr. Still's body retrievers. Sounds like a breed of dog, but what they did and how they did it was ultra-critical in starting the process of getting the body to its final resting place.

The van bobbed up and down now under Thad, his imagination in full-bloom, taking him into the future. A familiar feeling, no, something stronger than a feeling, a sense, because his imagined dead body heard the two men talking, but couldn't make out what they said. Their voices weren't distorted, just too low to make out. Scientifically, a strange thing, with Thad's head and ears not more than two to three feet away from where they sat.

But that intense sensitivity Thad experienced made sense of the science. It wasn't the physical distance between his ears and their voices. It was the distance between death, where Thad imagined he was, and life, which the two body retrievers still had. Yet, Thad existed. Whether it was his consciousness, spirit, or both, he was still *alive* somewhere. But where?

Whatever form or lack thereof, he existed. Just as those alive know they exist. Somehow, he was, simultaneously, far away, yet, never left Earth, still inside his body. Whether the part of him that remained in his body was a remnant to catch up with the rest later or, perhaps, would remain with the body, belonged to it, he didn't know. Until now, the idea that a part of the conscious or soul would stay back within the body had never occurred to him. Remain with the remains, as it were, ensuring death hadn't been cheated by giving it the body only instead of the whole package.

It seemed fair to Thad. The word *balance* kept coming to mind. What he didn't like was being in two places at once. This experience would haunt him for the rest of his days. If this was an actual glimpse into death, it wasn't what he expected.

Where was the glorious part about it? The better place everyone says it is?

As if the far away Thad had said to the one on Earth, Thad heard, *Think about who says such things.*

Immediately, Thad knew. *Those not dead yet.*

All three Thads questioned at once, *What would they know about death?*

Then, only the voice of Thad, the one not dead yet—only imagining it, lying in the death hauler, spoke, *Only that it happens.*

That was all Thad knew.

For all he knew, maybe that dual existence didn't last, and the conscious remnant in the body stopped existing, leaving only the part far away. And perhaps then, only then, the dead go to the better place and partake of all the good things about being dead.

Thad was searching again. Like those *other* people. And he was sweating. Speculative feelings and sensations had worked him up into a lather. Which meant the experience was total horseshit. Nothing to hang his hat on. He didn't know anything more than when he had laid down.

Thad sat up, slid out of the van, and closed its doors.

Heading for the refrigeration storage, where bodies were held for cremation or in case of a backlog, he peeked back at the van, wondering about his experience.

At the refrigerator, he opened the door. It was empty. How he wished it wasn't. On a couple of tours given by Mr. Still, there had been bodies stored inside. When the door opened, a smell of uncompromised death had escaped, despite the refrigeration.

Discreetly, Thad had breathed it in, deep and full. One time, one of the bodies had been in there for nearly three days. That one had seared his memory in both how it looked and smelled.

For nothing had been done to these bodies awaiting cremation. They weren't cleaned, embalmed, or anything. They didn't need to be, eventually being incinerated.

The smell of that body remained in Thad's nostrils for some time, he recalled. All of a sudden, out of nowhere, the smell would show up. A visitation from the dearly departed. So, not to be rude, Thad always made sure to breathe it in, amazed at how its aroma intensified the more he paid attention to it. It had been a long time since he had experienced that, but maybe that's what happened in the van.

There must not have been any cremations lately. Thinking about it, Thad knew there hadn't been. Gainell, Peachtree, and Lockie were all burials. Recalling names and services had taken Thad mentally back months into history's past before he could come up Mr. and Mrs. Elute, who had died together in a fishing boat accident.

The story was they took a boat out on the lake to fish without anyone knowing. Their kids grown and out of the house, days had passed before anyone realized they were missing. When their son had visited the house and no one was there, he contacted the authorities. The long and end of it was no one knew what had happened to the Elutes for a long time.

Then, some boys, playing near the water at the lake, came upon something they swore might have been a small whale or shark. They were too young to know what kind of life lived in and around the lake. All they knew was that whatever lay on the embankment had lived once. Had to, because it was flesh and blood, pale in color, and large. What threw them for a loop was this animal had strands of cloth around its body.

In the void spots where the cloth wasn't, gashes, gouges, and gaps of open flesh dotted and lined the body. A faint pink they were.

Later, it was determined it was Mrs. Elute, her body enlarged by bloating and being waterlogged. Once authorities identified the body, the search for her husband began. The morning they were to start looking, a hungover teen boy, who had partied with some friends the night before, had passed out on a different bank than where Mrs. Elute had been found. When he woke up, his head felt like it had been cracked open.

What he didn't understand was why the hell his face, arms, hands, and legs hurt. When he checked himself over, large, red domes covered nearly his entire exposed skin. Most of them had a tiny hole in the middle of them—a puncture point. Only where his clothes covered had been spared. Lying next to him was Mr. Elute's bloated, waterlogged, feasted-upon body.

Word has it, some of those bug and unknown bites had left permanent scars on the kid. He also never touched a drop of alcohol after that. No, sir, and ma'am—the Elutes had set him straight. Waking up beside a dead body was enough intervention to say the devil's poison couldn't be trusted.

Under the circumstances, the surviving family thought a closed-casket burial would be best. They even went as far as researching over-sized caskets for their parents' ballooned bodies. Yes, that's right. Coffins can be sized. And the over-sized option for large people is a booming business—with more people weighing in as obese.

In the end, the Elutes were cremated. Probably best—under the circumstances.

8

IN thinking about the Elutes' story, it occurred to Thad that he might die in a similar fashion. When he talks with Costa tomorrow, he'll mention planning for cremation just in case that would become the more prudent option.

To say the way to death is different for everyone would place the one who said it in the imbecile category. Too many people die from the same things. The big killers, heart disease and cancer, will claim the most. But even the way the Elutes had died could be classified as an unintentional accident, which also ranked up there.

Thad wouldn't mind venturing on a less-traveled path to death if possible. He made a mental note to make some lifestyle changes in hopes of avoiding heart disease, cancer, and others to increase his chances of dying from a cause much lower on the human killer list. Perhaps, being strangled by his own beard.

Thad didn't have a beard. So, he made another mental note to start growing one right away, long enough to strangle.

Then, Thad thought, *What if my death was so strange and bizarre that no one knew exactly* how *I died?*

Yes, he liked that. Screwy deaths where the exact cause wasn't clear always contained an aura of mystery. Disappearances were mysterious, but that wasn't what Thad wanted. Just because a person disappeared didn't mean they were dead. And just because they were never heard from again doesn't mean anything. Maybe they didn't want to be heard.

No, screwy had to tighten or loosen the screw. Removing the screw, like a disappearance, wouldn't leave any evidence. The screw needed to remain. Which meant the body needed to be found as evidence to confirm Thad had died. But, only the body without any other evidence, so no one could piece together what the hell happened to poor Thad E. Hadet.

Oh, if my name would live in infamy, Thad thought. *Like Amelia Earhart—but no disappearances!*

Planning for death is a bitch, he thought. *There's almost too much to plan. Too many contingencies. But I'll be ready. 'There's nothing more manly than a prepared man,'* Mr. Still had said.

Thad walked over and stood beside the hearse. Yes, the big black transporter of the dead. A whale, which carried the dead in its mouth. Jonah's whale from the book of Jonah in the Bible. A story about being swallowed by death, buried in the belly of a whale, graved in water, only to be resurrected—vomited into new life, perhaps eternity.

Not much different than being born— vomited out of a vagina, already bathed in blood.

He touched the hood, cool from not being moved. Not everyone knows about the whale, but everyone knows the hearse. You see it and immediately think of death. No matter if it's carrying a corpse, loved ones, or only a driver on his way to fill it with gas, we see it and are reminded of the inevitable. A dark angel, escorting the deceased to their final resting place. Perhaps, the Grim Reaper himself, seeing the task through until completion.

Thad walked around the vehicle as if checking out a new car on a dealer lot. In inspecting the automobile, the rear passenger tire appeared to be a little flat. He will inform Costa or Mr. Still when he came back tomorrow.

He stopped at a back window and touched it. Through his own reflection and of the garage behind him in the glass, no matter how hard he imagined, he didn't see anyone in the back seat. Everything else came in clear. The hearse strolling down Gateway Street toward Heaven on Earth Cemetary.

Thad shook his head like an Etch-A-Sketch to clear the image.

No one in the back seat? Not many cars behind the hearse? What's going on?

What was going on was Thad never married. Hell, he wasn't even dating. The details of the last date he went on were sketchy, but he could recall them if he wanted to—but he didn't. No kids. No siblings. Mother in one town over. His father had died three years ago from some kind of fungus that had infiltrated the coast of Florida while on a fishing trip. Screwy, that was. And different. Just the sort of death that people will be talking about for years to come—the deadly black gunk off Florida. Where did it come from? The depths of the ocean? Space?

Thad had some aunts, uncles, and other relatives he never really knew—a few nearby, most out-of-state. And a few friends who were mostly acquaintances.

And there it was, the writing on the proverbial wall.

Now, Thad was Thad and not King Belshazzar. Nor did he see a hand appear and start writing on the palace wall. Thad didn't own a palace; he rented an apartment.

Still, it was clear enough. In front of his face, as it were. And outside of his mother, no one else of significance stood there.

He made another mental note to work on that. People may not reciprocate, but he could try a little harder and stop being such a recluse.

How am I to die, playing it so safe?

Indeed. Another mental note to get out more where the danger was. Sure, there were plenty of things that could go wrong in the apartment, but chances of coming across something screwy, like the deadly black gunk off Florida, could only be found out and about.

Taking this tour alone without the distraction of Mr. Still had brought to the surface many things Thad had not considered before. The mental notes were stacking up to where maybe he should write them down.

To say he hadn't thought of his lonely life prior wasn't entirely accurate. Without question, this environment only amplified such thoughts. It was much easier to imagine the finality of life and all it meant here in the lingering presence of the departed. Who was teaching him from the grave how to be prepared before the Grim Reaper appeared before him unannounced, swung that scythe through him, and yanked his soul out of his body.

9

Now, Thad laid flat on his back in the back of the hearse, with his arms crossed over his chest and eyes closed, pondering many things. But one in particular that lingered was the lack of attenders at his future funeral. Assuming his mother would pass before him, there was no one else. No one to speak meaningful words. A minister from a church Thad never attended would be assigned—and paid—to say something. Oh, there would be the usual commending of his spirit into God's hands and care, but really, the minister would end up not saying anything. Not really. How could he, not knowing Thad from Adam.

As much as Thad had thought about death since twelve-years-old, it was becoming more apparent why people don't pre-plan their funeral arrangement. It's a goddamn neverending circle of worry. Just when you think you have it all the way you want it, something else not considered before whispers to you you're a dumbshit and gums it all up.

It's this place, Thad thought. *And the people in it. Not Mr. Still, Costa, Alice, or Gretchen. No, I mean Gainell, Peachtree, Lockie, the Elutes. The dead. They're the ones who were whispering.*

Lying in the back of the hearse, Thad heard exactly that—a whisper. *"You're taking this too far."*

10

THAD opened his eyes. The whisper had not been a figment of his imagination. It's true he possessed a vivid one. One that expressed itself through his senses and, yes, there were times he swore he had heard a noise, only not to hear it when he paused and listened carefully. This wasn't one of those times. For he *knew* he had heard it—audibly. And he knew what he had heard. *'You're taking this too far,'* someone had said.

Of course, the line between knowing something and thinking it can vary in width. Be assured; this wasn't a blurred line or a fine line, but a wide line. Broad, solid, and distinct enough to block out any gray.

So now what? He had heard a voice whisper to him inside the hearse. A voice with a message. *'You're taking this too far.'*

Taking what *too far?* Thad wondered.

Honestly, the only thing he could do was wait and see if he heard it again. Until then, he would continue on his tour.

After climbing out of the back of the corpse-carrying automobile, Thad headed for one of his favorite rooms in the funeral home: the embalming room.

When he opened the door, blue ultraviolet lights barely broke through the darkness, creating shadows on the two sinks, counter, carted-tray, adjustable table where the body laid, and the blood-sucking monster—the embalming machine.

Before entering, Thad stood there with the door open, taking in the view. A view that could only be described as confusing. On one hand, the blue UV lights created a heavenly aura in the room. On the other, a creepy suspicion inhumane things went on here, similar to those experimental therapy rooms in now-closed state hospitals where unconventional treatment methods oftentimes bordered on mental, emotional, and physical torture.

The staggering coincidences between those state hospital wings and rooms and the embalming room at a funeral home couldn't be denied. Sharp, surgical instruments. A body table. Strange machines with dials and tubes.

Thad sympathized with people who never wanted to see the inside of the embalming room until they had to. At which time, they would be dead and unable to see it with the physical eyes in their once occupied head. And it was highly unlikely anyone would see themselves in this room through spiritual eyes since the death always happened prior to bringing the corpse to this room.

Thad entered the embalming room and closed the door behind him without turning on any other lights. Even though this room and all others like it in funeral homes all over the globe contained both heavenly and hellish qualities, he knew it just wasn't so. By the time the body got to this point, any warring over the soul, if it existed, had been settled.

Not that the room lacked confusion. To say it didn't would be a lie. Is there anything more confusing than death? Without the accompaniment of Mr. Still, death did seem more confusing. A certain uncertainty. Standing there, Thad knew what bothered people the most about the embalming room and it went beyond what happened there. It had a lot to do with *who* was performing the procedures.

Oh, some come off macho, expressing once they're dead and gone they could care less about what happens to their body left behind. But deep down, they do. With the average cost of a funeral with burial or cremation around $8,500, damn right they do. And a large chunk of that money goes toward the final resting place: the plot, burial vault, gravemarker, and the casket. So, people can say what they want—and they do—but words are cheap. Actions always have and always will speak louder than words.

Another truth, how people spend their money and time says a lot about them and what they care about. And there was no denying that dropping $6,500—more than what most people have in a savings account—to ensure their body would rest comfortably underground proved people cared about the handling of their corpse after death.

In fairness, if anyone gave a damn about the departed, then the final resting place of the body or ashes would be visited more often. That alone made it important. Survivors had their lives to live and visiting a gravesite didn't have to be unsafe when it was already a major downer. Visited or not, where remains rest or ashes were scattered, that place becomes the departed's lasting memorial.

Thad's memorial would be in Heaven on Earth Cemetary.

For as long as it lasted, that is. Or the grave recycled. In a hundred years, maybe? Let's go with that, a nice round number. At which time, whether there were pieces of Thad's bones still in the coffin or not, the caretaker would be looking at recycling Thad's plot for someone else. Thad's remains would be stored below the recently dead's and the headstone would be etched on the opposite side with the newly dead's information and flipped around.

Hell, Thad wouldn't care if a new headstone was purchased as long as his information was on it somewhere. Because after all affairs had been settled and the dead person, too, they have, essentially, been erased from life. And outside the death certificate and other documents that remained hidden in storage, the only thing saying they ever lived was the minimal information engraved on the marker.

It never seemed enough to Thad. Or right, for that matter. After all the individual had lived through, the dead's last words came down to their name, date of birth, date of death, and a quote, phrase, saying, scripture, or something similar on the marker. For most, that was about it. Maybe their picture and an emblem if there was space.

Others are buried without words. Markers consisting of only a letter or number. Or no marker at all. Without question, there are more dead in the ground than markers above ground. The sea to even a greater extent. Nothing to say their bodies or sprinkled ashes journey had started there.

Some time ago, Thad had given Mr. Still a picture to use. A headshot to go on his upright headstone in the cemetery. It should still be in his file, but when Thad talks with Costa tomorrow, he'll check—just to make sure.

11

THAD walked over to the carted-tray. None of the instruments were on it, so he went to what he wanted to see the most—the embalming machine.

What Thad found so interesting about it was someone had conceived the initial idea of removing body parts and blood from the body before burial. Whether the Egyptians were the first to perform such procedures or an earlier people didn't matter. For Thad, it was that the idea to do something like that had entered a person's mind to begin with. And, as much as Thad was into this stuff, he knew that person's mind must have been either filled with the best intentions of burial respect to slow decomposition or, it suffered a sickness.

Where there didn't seem to be a middle ground, of course, there could have been. An upright citizen very well could have had their good intentions deranged slightly with just enough madness to come up with embalming.

Thad ran his fingers lightly over the machine, caressing it, as someone might a pet. They moved over the glass window of a gauge, then wrapped around a dial, feeling the grooves.

It always struck Thad in a weird way of how such a thought might have first come to someone. *How do I slow the body from rotting for the time it will be with the family until it was disposed of? I know. I know. It sounds a little crazy. Well, let's see. If I slice the body open and remove the organs, that should help. Oh, and can't forget that brain! But, I must keep those incisions to a minimum. That's it! I'll pull the brain out through the nose. No, the ears. No, not flexible enough. It must be the nose. Illogical, I know—through that small hole, but the mouth doesn't have a clear path. I'll make one. No, no. I must keep the incisions down. I'll drain the blood, too, while I'm at it. One of the main arteries should do. And water. Can't forget the water. The sun and a little salt should dry that up. I'll sprinkle some spices on the body to help with the smell. Maybe, some inside, too.*

Cutting, removing, cleaning, basting, spicing. Was the person a doctor or a chef? Not exactly sane thinking, but fascinating nonetheless. Perhaps, not so irrational with human cutlery skills on animals. They would be the same, wouldn't they? Flesh and blood were flesh and blood.

Sure—why not. But the confusion didn't stop there. Oh, no! Not for Thad inside the embalming room of a funeral home. Because the only thing separating such acts performed on a dead body from being allowed or being a felony, punishable by seven years imprisonment, depended on whether such actions were performed by a licensed authority or not.

For most people, that's not enough. Because professional embalmers are stereotyped as weird, morbid, and depressed. People persons, but the people need to be dead. They don't talk back. Or argue. Or look at you funny. And if they do, well—

Just the kind of job for Thad E. Hadet. If he

needed a job. Or wanted a job. Which he didn't on both accounts.

It had crossed his mind, of course. As much time as he had spent at the funeral home over the years, maybe he should have gotten paid for being there. But he would be busy with work and not have the freedom to imagine what it might be like to be dead.

While touching the tubes, Thad wondered if Alice would embalm him. She was only in her fifties, so it was possible.

Admirable work, she does, Thad thought. *A true servant to mankind, carefully preserving each one who came through here, while making them appear to be in a peaceful sleep to help comfort friends and family. Unappreciated, Alice is.*

Next time Thad sees her, he'll have to thank her—while he can.

His index finger traced the amber natural rubber tubing curled up beside the embalming machine. A strange texture it had. Not many things in this world felt like that. Rubber, but soft and pliable. These types of tubes always reminded him of intestines, only darker in color.

Alice had touched these, Thad thought.

He was lost now. In the aura of the blue light, touching the tube was almost sensual.

"Through this tube, the chemicals will enter

my body," he whispered.

He fingered the other tube curled up on the other side of the machine.

Two, he thought. *Always two.*

"The chemicals will push the blood out of my body and out this tube," he whispered.

In and out. Born to die. The circle of life—and death.

Not caring now whether anyone was watching him or not, Thad climbed up on the table and laid flat on his back. He crossed his arms over his chest and closed his eyes.

Yes, that's it, he thought. *I'm here—the day of my death.*

12

THAD imagined Alice, wearing a smock, gloves, and a cloth helmet with a plastic shield across its front, performing her duties.

While he was alive and could, he lowered his hands to his sides and touched the grooves running along the perimeter of the table.

Only faint sounds of Alice moving in her

smock, working, reached Thad. It was just the two of them.

And that scares people. The whole idea of being alone, beyond vulnerable in being dead, and not being able to protect their body any longer, not being there with it.

Assuming that was how it went. Either way, the embalmer, or anyone else at the funeral home for that matter, could do whatever they wanted to the corpses entrusted there.

Trust—or the lack thereof—nailed an unspoken fear people have when it comes to the handling and care of their body after they leave it.

There it was again. The ideology of the person or soul leaving the body after death. An idea Thad hoped was accurate. Less than a belief and nothing close to faith, this hope could be described as wishful thinking. No matter how humans came into being, he hoped a person's consciousness did not remain in an inactive, dead body. Trapped for eternity or however long the world existed. That would be about as cruel as nature could get.

Unless we dreamed, Thad thought, calming down. *Living in my mind, as it were.*

He lived there now.

Alice touched his neck with a couple of gloved fingers. Instantly, he felt naked, undressed out of his burial suit. He knew what she was about to do.

I trust you, Alice, Thad thought.

For she had already washed, massaged, and shaved his body.

Did Alice cap my eyes? Thad wondered.

In talking with Mr. Still, Thad was told that they use caps to keep the eyes closed instead of glue. It wasn't the main reason, but *a* reason Thad had decided on the Will B. Still Funeral Home to handle his after-death affairs instead of Cecil Niwog's Funeral Home, which used glue.

Thad tried opening his eyes. He couldn't; they wouldn't. He was there—on the death table.

Yet, how did he feel Alice's touch?

And that? It just happened. A pinch in his skin at the neck.

Thad went to open his mouth and couldn't. Matter of factly, it wouldn't. Alice had already sewn it shut.

The blade of the surgical knife, Thad had seen on one of the tours, had sliced through his skin without Alice putting forth much effort. Then he felt it slice through his inner flesh, tearing through interwoven fibers, spreading open his neck.

The pressure there increased as Alice worked

harder now, burrowing the blade deep into his neck.

Finding what she was looking for, the carotid artery, Alice pushed the knife down, digging in there, sawing the artery like a thick tree limb. It took effort, for Thad heard her working. Slicing into an artery wasn't easy. They are more resilient than people realize. But, no question, Alice had the strength and experience to get it done, as she had done all those other times.

It didn't feel like Alice had slit his throat. There weren't any sweeping swings of the blade. No, her concentration on one particular spot made it more of a stab.

Technically, it wasn't far-off. The incision wasn't that long, about an inch-and-a-half to two inches, and no more than a quarter-inch wide, but it was deep. About the shape and size a butcher knife would make.

Thad felt Alice's gloved fingers enter the incision and pull on his flesh and skin to widen the hole.

I trust you, Alice.

13

Alice must have spread the hole to the size she needed, because, Thad felt a finger burrow deep and pull on what he could only describe as a cord near the neck. It wasn't like anything he had ever felt before. But a student of such matters, he knew what she had done. She had pulled the carotid artery through the hole to make it easier to work with to begin embalming.

With the artery exposed, Alice fingered that area for a while. It was important that the artery be braced in a way that it wouldn't snap back inside the body and the needle displace. There would be one hell of a mess if that happened. A big ole blood mess—Thad's blood—all over the embalming room.

The room already had enough mystery and confusion associated with it; the last thing it needed was blood splattered everywhere. Not that it would bother Alice, other than she would have to clean it up. Nor would any outsiders be coming in. According to Mr. Still, people weren't bum-rushing the funeral home for tours.

No worry, Alice braced the artery securely, as she had done all those other times before.

More fingering and pressure by Alice in locating the jugular vein, which will be used to drain Thad's blood as the embalming fluid pushed it out.

Oh, that feels weird, Thad thought, feeling Alice insert the drain tube into his jugular vein.

Oh! Oh!

The metal tube sliding into Thad's carotid artery propelled this experience to a whole new level. Beyond physical. A spiritual level, perhaps. Whether the body was truly sacred or not depended a little on whether God existed or not and, in large part, how a person felt about the human body.

Had Thad's body been desecrated? Disfigured? Mutilated?

Some might say so. However, Thad and the law would not. The wounds might be severe, for Alice had exerted effort and force to make them but not in a violent, malicious way. She was just doing her job. And the law would agree.

So did Thad. *I trust you, Alice.*

A soft hum sounded in the room. An occasional clicking sound interjected over the top of it. Pressure in Thad's neck told him it was happening, the embalming itself.

Alice massaged his body some more. Her hands were strong and sure. They would stop, now and again, at particular spots and her fingers would rub hard there as if working out a kink in a muscle. This professional embalmer knew just the right areas to work.

Thad began to feel lightheaded. Habitually, he wanted to touch his head, but his hands didn't move. Just as he couldn't open his eyes or move his mouth.

I'm really here, he thought, giddy. *It's really happening.*

Just then, a liquid ran through his fingers, which rested inside the drain grooves around the perimeter of the table.

Aah, Thad mentally sighed. *My blood.*

The watery-blood quenched his dry fingers.

Which wouldn't be far from the truth. He knew he would not look like he did now when this went down for real. More like a shriveled prune, a partially decomposed corpse dug up from the grave. Or climbed out. A flesh sack of bones. Skeletal with skin and not much meat in-between.

Alice saw Thad's fingers in the fluid, lifted his hands out of the channel, wiped them off, and set them beside his body on top of the table.

It doesn't matter how I look, Thad thought. *Or how any of the others had looked. Alice cared for us just the same.*

Maybe I should get to know her a little. In this life. A caring friend today, a caretaker tomorrow.

Thad couldn't raise his body or open his eyes to see it, but he knew the clear chemicals inside the receiving tank had probably already turned pink with his blood and would only shade to a darker red.

My blood no longer blood, Thad thought. *Contaminated. Mixed with some kind of chemical. Or chemicals. Mr. Still had said on the tours, but for the life of me, I can't remember.*

Mixed now, my blood and whatever Mr. Still had called biomedical and chemical waste. I remember him bitching about the cost of such removal. Alice was around that day. She had reminded him that properly handling such material and having it removed was unavoidable. The only way for him not to incur the cost was to get out of the funeral home business. Costa didn't care one way or the other. 'I just pay the bill,' I recall him saying.

They're all good people here. Each has a role to play. But none more important than Alice.

Thad reflected on his statement. *Are they good people? Or is business just business to Mr. Still? A job just a job for Costa? None more convenient than for Gretchen next door. And what about Alice?*

This whole time Thad had praised her.

It's true, Mr. Still wanted the business, so fellow-freemason Cecil Niwog's funeral home at the other end of town didn't get it. Nor did he want Gretchen going over there, either. It's also true that Costa Lot tacked on as many of Mr. Still's *incidentals* as he could without being obvious.

Take, take, take.

When a person dies, they are, for all intents and purposes, erased from life. Apartments are cleaned out. Utilities shut off. Possessions disbursed, donated, or trashed. Accounts closed. Insurances halted.

So, what about Alice?

Just when Thad had thought Alice's hands were clean, she's the one getting her hands dirty at this funeral house. For she was a taker, too. A taker of blood. A swiper of water. A shriveller of body mass. A sealer of eyes. A sewer of mouths. And Thad knew that wouldn't be all. Alice was about to take more.

14

ABOUT thirty minutes had passed and Thad's blood had stopped flowing in the drain-ditch molded around the perimeter of the body-table.

Thad knew what was coming next, but without the use of his eyes and body, he wouldn't know *when* it was coming.

As Alice continued to work, his imagination

ran wild, trying to associate sounds to create pictures of what she was doing. The anticipation of knowing what was coming but not knowing when scared yet excited him at the same time.

Some time passed and Thad had begun to wonder if Alice had switched up the usual sequence and had already done it or if this was going to be one of those caught-in-the-act of skipping a procedure that ought to be done.

I hope Alice wouldn't do that, Thad thought. *No matter if Mr. Still had told her to or not. Cutting corners wasn't the way…*

Whoa, Alice!

Something had punctured through his belly into his stomach. Alice did not forget to embalm his cavity. Nor was she exactly gentle with this particular invasive procedure.

The *something* that had plunged into his stomach was a long, hollow needle called a trocar. Thad felt the tip of it poke and prod around the inside of his stomach. Thoroughly, too.

So, more for the taking, Thad thought. *Alice's heart must be set on getting as much of me as she could.*

Meaning gas, fluid, and feces.

Take! Take! Take! Even my last meal.

Alice had prodded and sucked for some time.

I hope I don't feel any of this on the actual day. Once was enough.

After draining Thad's stomach and filling it with a solution, Alice moved on to the other organs in his body cavity, doing the same.

Not taking, Thad thought. *Replacing. An exchange of contents with chemicals.*

I'm sorry, Alice. Forgive me for being so cynical.

Nearly the entire inside of his torso felt sore from the poking, prodding, and sucking.

It's not your fault, Alice. You're just doing your job.

More than any other organ, his stomach felt full. Waterlogged. Like he had drunk a bunch of water. Gallons of it. And, in some ways, he had. Only it wasn't water. But formaldehyde mixed with other chemicals. And it just wasn't in his stomach, but also in his intestines.

A strange sensation on his stomach threw him for a loop. Concentrated. Pulling. Invasive.

I had forgotten about that, Thad thought, embarrassed, hating to admit it.

The plastic trocar button was being screwed into the puncture hole the trocar had made. He felt it now, unmistakable.

So much to remember. Thank goodness for the Alices of the world. They remember.

Alice remembered everything. All tasks, including unmentioned details, which Alice had completed so far to prepare Thad's dead body for services and burial, had gone smoothly. Focused and business-like she had been in doing them. And that was acceptable to Thad. In no way shape or form could he fault her for that kind of approach.

Well, maybe he had when he had thought of her as a taker—*Take! Take! Take!* But he was wrong, thinking now how it must be for Alice. To do what she does day-in and day-out and not be an absolute wreck was nothing less than remarkable. It's true; there was no chance of her killing a body twice. No pressure on that point. But to say there wasn't any pressure would be a flat-out lie.

Sure, everything done to the body after death fell nothing short of traumatic. The invasiveness. Poking. Prodding. Pulling. Draining. Filling. Stuffing. Gluing. Suturing. Cleaning. All to ensure the surviving family, friends, and respect-payers aren't traumatized by a leak, a smell, a spot of blood, a collapse, a raised bump, a disfigurement. To make a dead body appear as normal as possible days after death and, on top of that, make it appear to be peaceably at rest in the casket after everything done to it, required mad skills to accomplish.

Mad! A haunting hint, perhaps. Someone would have to be to do this type of work. Even

Alice, who had acquired the skills over the years to make the dead appear asleep. A rare breed, unfazed by the great unknown beyond death. A not-so-rare craft from millennia ago. About as ancient as humankind.

Time passed. How long, Thad wasn't sure. Alice's touches occurred less frequently.

Alice must be checking me over, Thad figured. *Inspecting me, making sure I'm presentable to the living.*

Then, hearing snaps from Alice removing both gloves, followed by a clackety sound Thad took as Alice removing her visored helmet, he assumed he had passed inspection.

I'm fit-to-be-tied, Thad thought, in thinking of Alice tying-off the veins earlier. The opposite of its traditional meaning, this had brought on a smile—or an attempt to smile, which never formed on Thad's stuffed, sewn mouth. And when it failed to form, that angered him a little.

Not enough to ruin his mood. Besides, what could he do about it anyway? Gratitude for Alice's efforts prevailed.

Thank you, Alice, Thad thought, wishing he could express it to her, so she knew. *I'm glad it was you.*

After experiencing first-hand what the dead can't communicate—only Alice and those like her can but very few care to listen—Thad felt blessed to have gone through it, but couldn't lie, he was glad it was over. When it happens for real, he'll be dead and won't feel a damn thing.

Hope springs eternal, anyway. It was *too* realistic, even for him. Most of the blessed feeling he had was because he could walk away from it.

No interest in lying there anymore to imagine having makeup applied and his hair combed, Thad went to sit up—but couldn't.

15

MAYBE Thad couldn't walk away from this. Hell, he couldn't even sit up to walk away.

Whoa! What was that?

Lightheadedness lifted his head into the clouds. Heaven, perhaps. Or so it seemed. Because his head never left the body-table in the embalming room.

Was this real? Am I dead? Is this really happening?

What else could he conclude? The evidence could not be denied. The lightheadedness he felt was from his blood being drained.

The dead don't touch, taste, see, talk, or hear.

But Thad could hear. And think. So, what does that mean?

I'm alive and *dead. How can that be?*

Fair question. However, the only person he could ask was himself, and he didn't know the answer. All along, he had planned for death—not being *alive* in death.

So, now what? Exactly, num-num, now what?

"*You're taking this too far,*" someone whispered.

It wasn't Alice, Thad knew. It was the same voice from inside the hearse.

But how could he explain it? A faint, echoey whisper, male, that sounded—

Ghostly, Thad concluded.

He no longer heard Alice. Maybe she was doing something quietly or waiting. Or maybe she had left the room. And left him all alone with—

Death.

Does *Death* really exist? Of course, it does. Time is spent. Judging how it was spent has no bearing. Because no matter how it was spent, living things start dying at birth. And from then on, who is there to collect from every living creature every millisecond that passes? *Death*.

Before any living thing knows it, they're broke. No more time, no more life.

But what about *Death* from that moment on? When life ceases, assuming there is more after, are they the same *Death*?

"Too far, Thad."

It knows my name, Thad hated to acknowledge. *Death knows me. I must be dead.*

Then, he realized that *Death* had already known him. From birth, the *Collector* had walked side-by-side with him during his life, patiently silent.

I never knew Death was there, Thad thought. *As much as I have thought about it, I never knew.*

Taking what too far, Thad mentally asked, thinking what could he lose if he was dead—if it was *Death* talking to him.

"This," the ghostly voice whispered.

Define this for me, Thad thought, carefully. *Is it death? Are you…*

"Those who long for death can bring it about prematurely."

Is that what I had done? Brought death earlier than it should have?

"Not entirely. You crossed over, Thad. Through powerful mental, physical, and emotional suggestions, your spirit desires to agree with your wishes."

Crossed over? So, I am dead.

"Not entirely. Your body isn't dead. Only mentally have you crossed the line."

Into another death?

"Dead is dead. Death still walks with you. Your consciousness has walked ahead into the void."

How do you know such things? There's only one way you would know. And that is if...

"Don't, Thad," the echoing whisper interrupted.

But I must!

"Don't."

Are you Death?

The whispering voice moaned in agony as if in pain. But flesh and blood never leave the Earth. No, the physical remains in the physical world. That was certain. The body buried, cremated—if there was a body. When not, then it was absorbed by the Earth. Outside of remains launched into space, human dust mostly returns to the dust of the Earth.

It took Thad mentally crossing over to hear the voice.

Now, its moans intensified into deep wails as if the voice had a physical form that could be harmed. They sounded excruciating. Like nothing Thad had ever heard spew out of a human or animal before. As if the owner of the voice was being burned alive.

Scared and confused, Thad yelled in thought, *Are you* Death*?*

A high-pitched squeal answered, challenging what his eardrums could handle and rang his head like a bell.

Then, there was more than one. *A legion of Deaths?* How many, Thad couldn't tell. He knew if he could cover his ears, it wouldn't have done any good.

They all sounded like whatever they experienced went beyond the highest level of pain, another realm of torture conceived by the worst evil.

Like they were all burning, Thad thought, remembering Nazi incinerators. *Trapped inside an inferno, yet, the fire wouldn't consume them.*

The pitch intensified, unbearable in Thad's ears; the number of them, the voices, possibly *Deaths*—beyond his own belonging to other people, must be growing. And there was no relief for them, nor Thad.

Mentally, Thad screamed as loud as he could, *STOP! Please! Just stop! I can't take it! I don't care if you are Death or not!*

Immediately, the wailing stopped.

A lingering reverberation rattled Thad's

head.

After a few moments of silence, Thad thought, *Are you still there?*

"I'm still here," a lone voice whispered. "I'm always here."

What was happening to you?

"Don't ask."

This time, Thad dropped it, learning his lesson. As much as he would have loved to ask all of the questions he had rehearsed and committed to memory just in case there happened to be a Supreme Being on the other side of this life, he knew the whisperer would not answer.

Whether he could or couldn't didn't matter. There was only one question to ask that mattered at this moment, so Thad asked it.

How do I get back?

16

THE voice whispered, "All you have to do, Thad, is long to return to life." Then, lower than a whisper, the voice added, sounding farther away, "*Your* life, Thad. Your *liiiiife.*"

As the echoing word *life* faded out, Thad felt a peculiar sensation throughout his entire being. Easily the strangest thing he had ever experienced. It was as if all of his non-physical stuff: his consciousness and all related mental capacities, emotions, and, yes, even his spirit seemed to flicker inside his body. Quick disappearances and reappearances. Like an unsure filament inside a light bulb.

Only this felt more violent. A jarring went along with the flicker. Life returning to his unmoving body. And pain. The non-physical kind. A second birth. And just about all births are violent and painful. Bringing forth life was never easy.

Odd, how Thad had never felt himself slip away. In the same way he had never sensed Death nearby, escorting him throughout his days. But the comeback was a bitch. In heat, by the way, because Thad's return came in hot.

Funny how he had returned in a flash when he swore he only contemplated returning at best. Hesitation and uncertainty kept him in neutral. Arguments for and against returning to his old life canceled each other out. As far as he was concerned, he never moved off the spot. Paralysis by analysis, not moving along anywhere. If he longed at all, it sure wasn't strong, intense, or powerful by anyone's definition.

So, why did I return so quickly? Thad wondered.

Hell, he didn't know he was back any more

than he had any idea of his departure. Ignorant of the whole thing.

Besides, there was no proof either had happened. Perhaps, his imagination had created the scenario, so he played along to the tilt. That would explain why he couldn't see, talk, or move.

Was it possible my imagination had also created the voice?

Thad knew it was. Plenty of times, he had heard voices in his head sound exactly how he had imagined.

Come to think of it, Thad recalled, *that voice that spoke to me sounded awfully familiar.*

Meaning what? The familiarity stemmed from using his imagination? The voice sounding exactly as he had imagined it would?

That would explain it. Only, when Thad had laid on the body-table in the embalming room, his mind only imagined what it would be like being dead, not about hearing a voice.

But his imagination was powerful enough to cross into death.

There wasn't even a glancing thought of hearing God's voice. Although he was dead— or at least pretending to be dead—he figured God never spoke to him during his life, so why would he start now in death.

Not that he believed in God. And most of

that unbelief grew into a belief that God didn't exist each time he had tried speaking to him and never heard anything back or saw any results from what he had expressed.

After a while, Thad stopped trying. Unanswered prayer killed the whole God-thing decisively. With most of the world falling into the unbelief or indifferent categories, Thad could only assume that meant a vast majority of prayer went unanswered, also assuming a majority in the world had tried communicating with the Almighty.

Thad E. Hadet had *had it*. Way up past the top of his head to where he was drowning. He could have kept swimming in that muck, but it was exhausting. Many times, the idea of stopping and letting the water swallow him had crossed his mind—which had done its own crossing. So did swimming to the bottom to pull the plug to drain the pool, for the God-pool is deep.

Finally, Thad settled on getting out of the pool. And, as most do, rather than assume God's an asshole and cared nothing for him, or worse, God cared for others by answering their prayers and ignored his, he simply stopped swimming and adopted an indifferent ideology to God.

Of course, his indifference fell under

unbelief, because fence-riding was always bullshit. Grow a pair and make a stand. Either you're in or you're out.

Thad had exited the pool some time ago—at the age of twelve.

Before Thad realized it, he was sitting up on the body-table in the embalming room.

17

AFTER checking himself over and testing his capabilities, in particular, his sight, then speaking, which proved his hearing, Thad hopped off the table to ensure his mobility, having mixed feelings about being back. Which confirmed, in its own right, that he was indeed back and alive. Because, most days, he lived with mixed feelings about being alive.

In checking his watch, not as much time had passed as he would have guessed, which was okay with him. But one thing was certain: today's tour was over. Oh, yeah. For one of the first times in a long time, Thad had to get the hell out of there.

It wasn't because of the experience. In fact, it was the opposite. It seemed so real. Then, to come out of it alive was, well, disappointing.

Feeling something, he jabbed the tip of his index finger into his ear and wiggled it. When he had lowered his hand, there was blood on it.

Yet, after all of that eardrum-busting screaming, no one in the funeral home had come in to check on him—because they never heard it.

Not entirely sure what had happened, it was best he got out of there for a while.

But, something did happen, Thad knew.

On his way out of the Will B. Still Funeral Home, which he appreciated the name now more than ever after that experience, he ran into Gretchen.

"Oh, hey, Gretchen. You're here early," Thad said.

"Yeah," Gretchen said. "My husband's sick, so I thought I'd come in early so I can get back."

"Sorry to hear that. I hope it's nothing serious."

Now, this is going to sound about as messed up as thinking can get, but Thad was all ears, waiting for Gretchen's answer. Because if she happened to say it *was* serious, it crossed his mind to ask if it was contagious. Because, if it was, he just might have to pay her husband a visit. With Death collecting the time it took to walk every step.

Not that Thad gave a damn about Gretchen's husband. Not at all. Hell, he might take that chance Mr. Still had suggested earlier when he said, *'I also know you ain't a queer. I've seen you checking out Gretchen in here. You should take the chance and go over there while her husband's at work and see if she'll let you enter her spa for an oil massage—if you catch my meaning.'*

Thad knew the meaning. Mr. Still might have phrased it as only the stale fart could, but he knew. And this time, there was no way for her husband to find out. That is if Thad waited until after his departure.

No, this visit would serve only one purpose. And that would be to see if he could catch whatever her husband had.

That would get me back on that body-table for real, he thought. Which, of course, would also kill the possible start-up with Gretchen. *Maybe she'd*

*agree to a pity-lay before whoever or whatever sent me
back to the embalming room.*

Twisted, Thad knew, but these were twisted times. Things of this world were all goofed up. And there were worse things than having a death fetish.

'Those who long for death can bring it about prematurely,' the unknown voice had said.

"Thad. Did you hear a word I said?" Gretchen asked.

"Oh, *um,*" Thad started, embarrassed. "I'm sorry. No. I guess I have a lot on my mind."

She rubbed her hand along his arm in sweeping, caring strokes.

"It's okay. We all suffer from overstuffed brains."

Thad tried remaining relaxed to hide his excited heart, heavy breathing, to stop sweat from forming on his face, as well as the redness.

It had been a long time since he had been touched by a woman—a very long time. Alice would have been the last—only that wasn't real. He would have to go all the way back to a doctor's visit at the beginning of the year.

Sure, there was the occasional glancing brush in taking pets from their owners like Mrs. Dray at the apartment, but Gretchen reached out to him and voluntarily stroked his arm.

When he went to speak, a loud gulp preceded his words, which embarrassed him more, then he squeaked out, "You were saying."

"Thank God, it's nothing serious," Gretchen explained. "I don't know what I would have done if it was. We've been together for such a long time."

In remembering that time, her hand remained on Thad's arm, but no longer stroked it.

Thad stepped back. "Well, that's good news. I'm happy for you."

It was easy for her to see the irritation. "*Yeah*, me…"

"Hey, Gretchen," he interrupted. "I want to ask a favor of you if I could. A *big* favor."

Hesitantly, she said, "I'll try. What is it?"

"Tonight, say eleven-ish, would it be possible for you to walk back over here and let me in?"

18

OF course, Gretchen wanted to know why. And after Thad had explained, she felt sorry for him. If Mr. Still ever found out, he wouldn't like it, but knowing Thad and his ways, the old man wouldn't be shocked. Many times, the old coot had said he liked having Thad around, that it was good for business. The appearance of busyness in doing business. And, in some ways, Thad was like a part of the staff. He was their unofficial product-tester, trying them out before being used and even provided reviews. Mr. Still would take notes of what Thad liked and didn't, which came in handy in making recommendations, which turned into sales. All for free, which Mr. Still liked.

So, believing this wouldn't result in Mr. Still canning her, Gretchen agreed. Besides, what would it hurt? One way or another, Thad would find a way in anyway, so why turn this into a legal circus.

Thad thanked Gretchen and stepped forward with his arms open to hug her, but in seeing it, she shied away. It hurt, Thad couldn't lie, but he never got mad. Tonight, this woman was going to get out of her comfy bed and leave a warm house to let him in—a favor he would never forget.

About to unlock the door to his apartment, Thad heard a scratchy, "Oh, Thaddeus," come from down the hall. The voice was unmistakable.

Turning around, Thad said, "Hello, Mrs. Dray. How was your tea?"

"Oh, fine. Just fine," Mrs. Dray said with a little unbelief in her words.

Returning to unlock his door to get inside, he said, "Well, good. I'm glad everything worked out."

A bubbly laugh popped from the woman. "Oh, I wouldn't go that far."

The farther, the better, Thad thought.

"Oh," slipped out of his mouth. A mistake. A colossal one. Never, ever show interest.

Too late—he had. Undoable as they say.

Mrs. Dray went on and on about her *'unrestful'* day with her cat Muncie.

Hearing about all he could stand, Thad worked on opening his door and interrupted, "I'm sorry to hear that, Mrs. Dray, but there are things I need to do this afternoon and evening. Please excuse me."

As he stepped through the door, that grating whine scratched his ears when she asked, "Can you watch Muncie tomorrow?"

And there it was. Obvious from the get-go.

"No, Mrs. Dray," he answered. "I'm terribly sorry, but I'm going away tonight and won't be back until later in the day."

"Well, what time…"

"I don't know, Mrs. Dray. Whenever I damn well feel like it."

"Well, I never."

"Neither do I, anymore. Goodnight, Mrs. Dray. I'll be in touch to let you know when I'll be around to watch Muncie."

As he closed the door and locked it, the old woman mumbled on the other side before leaving him be.

Already dressed in the suit he was to be buried in, Thad went to the bathroom to check himself over. Beard not bad. A wet comb through the hair to freshen it up. A splash of cologne. Good enough. Tonight was only a trial run. Besides, when the real moment came, Alice would have him looking about as good as a dead person could.

Turning out the bathroom light and wandering through the apartment into the kitchen, he turned on the light and opened the fridge.

Nope, he rejected the idea. *The dead don't lay in a coffin with a full stomach. Oh, no, they don't. Not ever. Their bellies are emptied by the trocar. Even their last meal is taken from them.*

He closed the refrigerator door, turned off the light, went to the living room, and sat on the edge of the couch.

Suit a little wrinkly.

He didn't want to wrinkle it more by sitting back. It occurred to him he could have removed his coat until it was time to leave, but why bother. It was only a trial run.

That's twice now, he thought, referring to *'trial*

run.'

It was all he had thought about for the next hour—the whole idea of what if the *trial run* turned into the real deal. The headline in the paper would read,

Man wearing suit found dead in coffin inside funeral home

Erect and perfectly still, Thad had sat there, waiting, only moving once to go to the bathroom. It reminded him of the embalming table.

All of that would be out. Alice would make sure of it. Human waste has no place inside the dead body. Nor inside the coffin.

In checking the time, he had about a quarter of a day to wait. There were other things he could be doing, but *waiting* seemed right, acceptable, how every living thing should exist.

At least he wasn't alone. Because, unlike experiences before the one today in the funeral home, he sensed *Death* sitting beside him, also *waiting*—and collecting his dwindling life.

19

AT eleven o'clock, Gretchen had snuck out of the house and walked over to the funeral home. Letting Thad in was as far as she would participate in this lunacy. No way was she giving him a key. Knowing him, he would get copies made and end up living there—more than he already had. All along, she felt he spent too much time there. *Unhealthy*, she always said.

Before leaving him, Gretchen added, "This is already weird, but nothing too weird, okay. Promise me, Thad."

"Have any new corpses come in?" Thad said. "Of the female persuasion?"

It was hard for her to tell whether he was joking or not. Then, a hint of a smile appeared on his deadpan face.

She smiled, too. "No," Gretchen said. The smile went away. "*See!* Forget it. I'm not doing it. I knew you would take this too far."

"Why does everyone think that? I'm joking. *Come on!* You know I was joking, right?"

"Well ... I don't know. When's the last time you been laid?"

Unexpected, the question coming from Gretchen. It turned Thad on. Her touch earlier and question now had curled his right testicle over the trigger of his already loaded squirter about to fire. Enough to soak through his underwear and wet his pants. He would have to postpone tonight. Get his suit cleaned and try again.

There wouldn't be another tonight, Thad knew. He had to disarm this ticking timebomb. Thankfully, his mother came to mind; the testicle came off the trigger and retreated.

Good thing. Time was tight as it was and not

a sliver could be spared on a married woman.

Thanks, Mom.

"Has it been that long, you have to think about it?" Gretchen pushed.

"Well, *um*, let's see," Thad started. "*Laid? Hmm.*" Thad's face crinkled small. "You just came right out and asked it, *huh.*" He shook his head. "*Laid!*—Well, I don't think that's any of your business."

With attitude, she shifted her weight to her other leg and stated firmly, "It is, or you can forget about tonight."

"Tonight," he said, almost too quick. "Then, *yes.* I have slept with someone recently."

"So, who was the lucky lady?"

"*Unt-uh!* No way am I telling you…"

"Goodnight, Thad," Gretchen said, turning and walking toward the house.

"Mrs. Dray," Thad answered.

Gretchen turned around. "Mrs. Dray? The cat woman you're always telling me about."

"Yes," Thad answered, lifting his chin. "That's why I talk about her so much."

"There's, *what*, a twenty-year difference between you two?"

"Age doesn't matter. You should know that."

"I know, but … I don't believe you."

"Okay, then. How about this?" Thad girded

himself and said, "I love her. We're in love. She loves me and," he motioned a finger that it was a two-way street, "I love her. Mutually. A mutual love. We love each other."

"Eloquently put. What about her cat?"

"A triangle, then." Thad snapped his fingers and pointed at her. "A *love* triangle."

"So, the cat participates in this love?"

Gretchen was making him crazy. *Mother! Oh, Mother!*

Thad tilted his head. "Sometimes. When it's right. When it feels like an appropriate time to bring that kind of furry feature into it."

"I married the wrong man."

Thad nodded. "Yes. Yes, you did." He spread his hands. "Still available, if you're ever," he coughed, "interested."

"My husband would kill you," Gretchen pointed out.

Sick, but the thought had crossed Thad's mind.

"How do you suppose he would he do it?" Thad asked.

"*For God sakes, Thad!* You have serious issues. You know that, don't you?"

"Can't we go inside, please? It's chilly out here."

Weather's cold and Gretchen's dirty talk had brought on cold sweats.

"Oh, God," she whispered to herself. "Why not just stay out here and freeze to death?"

Thad cocked his head, then straightened it. "I didn't think of it."

Shaking a finger at him, she said, "See, you're not thinking straight. How can I trust you when your mind is bent? That was a test, Thad. And you failed. You should have said, *Gretchen, it won't work. The temperature is above freezing.*"

"I'm sorry, I…"

"You know what, you've already got an arm in a straight-jacket, so … I guess … what's the difference."

We're both halfway gone, Gretchen. About midway, in fact. Half paid up, if not more.

"Thank you, Gretchen," he said. "I'll never forget it."

Unlocking the door, she said, "Well, you better, for both our sakes," and let him in.

20

Tonight was, perhaps, the most important night in Thad's life. Forget night; *time* would be more accurate. Thad had to do this. Just had to. Not only to experience what he wanted to experience but also to see if the voice—Death's voice—would return to say more.

Thad flipped on a light, then turned it off.

No one could say for sure, but he believed death was dark. That the human spirit didn't emit light or glow as usually depicted. Nor was there a heaven with the father and son's light reflecting off crystal seas and streets of gold. To him, death without physical eyes had to be dark and spiritual eyes don't exist.

Going through the funeral home in the dark wasn't a problem. Thad knew the layout better than his tiny apartment. Besides, he knew exactly where he was going.

Standing beside the Spanish-Gray casket in the showroom, he ran both hands over the cover, feeling its smoothness.

A shame, really, Thad thought. *It's too pretty to be buried in dirt.*

Costa!

He had almost forgotten—the casket switch wasn't official. He hadn't met with Costa, yet. Why he had associated the *man* with *soil* was unlike him. Maybe a preemptive conclusion that the additional $500 for his latest casket selection would probably stick.

I'll leave him a note. Just in case something happens tonight.

As soon as he had thought it, he felt stupid.

Then, they'll know I've been in here. Mr. Still will question everybody, including Gretchen. And what will she say when put on the spot?

An idea came.

Think, Thad. Were they here when I left earlier? No. I don't think either one was here. They were out to lunch. A long one. Well into the afternoon. But they would have seen it when they came back.

Costa wouldn't care. He might not even remember or think twice about it. The only thing he cared about this place was the paycheck.

Thad settled he would leave Costa a note, expressing his wishes for this particular casket and see what he could do about reducing the extra $500.

A waste of time, he knew. If something goofy happened tonight, the full difference and more would be coming out of his estate because, with him no longer around to argue the point, there was no way Mr. Still or Costa would do him a solid.

After turning on the light of Costa's office and writing the note, making sure to mention the model, referencing the one on display in the showroom, the Spanish-Gray colored one with white material inside, he laid it on Costa's desk.

Another thought came to mind, so Thad picked up the pen and added to the note about wanting Costa to plan and price-out a back-up cremation plan not to exceed his current one, just in case he died similar to the Elutes and cremation would be the better option.

About to turn off the light and leave Costa's office, Thad turned back around and thought, *Over the years, I've made requests to Mr. Still and Costa, but I've never checked my file to ensure everything was correct.*

It was true. Not once had he ever gone through his file—a potential funeral-ruining laziness on his part. People make mistakes. They also forget. He might have died with inaccurate information in his file and the funeral would have been a disaster.

Everything about a funeral was important. And not just to Thad. There were others like him all over the world. Those who long for death. He had read about them. Even thought about getting in touch with a couple of them. But, he never did.

Again, all aspects of a funeral should be planned with the utmost care. *Last wishes* pull on the heartstrings of family and friends, usually trying their best to remember what the departed had wanted at their funeral. Flowers. Music. Pictures. Video. Who would perform the services. Clothing. Casket. Any special insignia or words on the inside material or on the corpse-container itself.

There's a lot to plan for, Thad reminded himself.

There was. Thad wasn't making something out of nothing. *Last wishes* were no joke. Nor was the memory of the funeral for those left behind.

Take color coordination. Sure, most funerals start and end with black. The dead are dressed in black. Those attending wear black. Black was a given, signifying a dark, sad day in people's lives. But, never discount those splashes of color in the forms of flowers and other ancillaries in the backdrop. While some of these should be planned, especially when fulfilling the departed's *last wishes*, the rest shouldn't and happen naturally. Usually, such items are brought by those attending the funeral and their freedom of choice must be allowed. A balance between the departed, dead pale in black, and the attenders in living color must be achieved. Never forget, the dead and living are present together in numerous places and under innumerable circumstances, but a funeral and burial are the final meetings between the two.

No doubt, Thad took death seriously and everyone else should, too. *Death* does. Besides, for Thad and those who long for the afterlife, planning wasn't only smart, but it also consumed some time while he waited. A lot of time.

There was no guesswork as to where Costa kept his file. Thad knew exactly where to find it. For Costa had pulled it enough times in his presence, usually making a comment like, "Quite a file we have on you, Mr. Hadet," from it being much thicker than other files.

Thad pulled his file from the filing cabinet and began reviewing his information. (The headshot photo of himself was there.) It excited him. So much so, that if he kept going, he might not sleep tonight. Which would put the kibosh on why he was inside the Will. B. Still Funeral Home at eleven-thirty at night.

I'll review it in the morning before anyone gets in, Thad planned, leaving his file open on Costa's desk.

Remembering something else, he picked up the pen and added to the note that the rear passenger tire on the hearse looked a little flat. About as organized as he could be, he set the pen down on top of the letter, turned off the light, and left.

21

ONCE more, Thad stood beside the Spanish-Gray casket in the dark showroom. For a while, he stood there, feeling the white, silky fabric.

Strange, but a part of him didn't want anything to happen to him tonight. There were too many loose ends. The casket change. A backup cremation plan. No, he had to live to make sure they were set up correctly.

I want to live?

It was strange, thinking such a thought. For most of his life, Thad had thought the opposite. Since twelve-years-old. Most of his life. Now, he wanted to live?

Not really. And not entirely. Only a part. A small part. The anal-retentive part that wanted everything planned out in detail.

But, I won't be there to make sure everything was carried out as I had requested. All of the planning might end up being just that—planning.

Every time he thought like this, it made him conclude that life could be summed up by one word—vanity. With the wisdom of King Solomon, deep down, he knew the best-laid plans were just that—plans. Execution was altogether a different matter. And success coming from those plans was, well, something a very small percentage of people find.

Thad couldn't worry about it. Sneakily, Death was busy at work, collecting his life-time.

Then, as if Thad had made up his mind, or the timing was right, or deciding there wasn't any time to waste, he climbed into the corpse-box with an urgency that even caught him off-guard.

Situated, lying in the casket, he asked himself, *Why the hell did I do that?*

Not concerning getting inside the coffin, because that was why he had come here tonight. Rather, why the sudden urgency to climb inside? It wasn't like he didn't have all night to do it. There wasn't a precise timetable for this test. He could have gotten in earlier or even later than now. Really, it didn't matter, as long as he logged enough hours inside the coffin to decide if it was what he truly wanted.

Eternity, if the Earth lasted that long, was a long time to lay in one spot. So, he figured, a good night's rest or a horrible one was the ultimate way to test the casket.

Most may find this to be a little extreme or even supreme-extreme. But, for those who long, spending a night inside a coffin was a small sacrifice to learn of its comfortableness.

Perhaps, the greatest sacrifice in finding out this information was what people would say if anyone ever found out. And that would depend on whether Gretchen opened her mouth or not.

I trust you, Gretchen, Thad reaffirmed to himself, much in the same way he had trusted Alice in the embalming room. So, there was no sense in worrying about being called a vampire, suicidal, a corpse-banger, or one morbid Satanist son-of-a-bitch possessed by devils.

Call me, Legion! Thad didn't care. Name-calling wouldn't hurt as long as he didn't let it. The truth was what he cared about the most.

The voice.

Ah, yes. Another truth Thad wouldn't mind getting to the bottom of.

Who was it? Death? Why talk to me?

An excitement quickened him. Something occurred to him he hadn't thought of before.

Was my death coming soon? Thad pondered, hoped. *'You're taking this too far,'* the voice had said. *Although I had made it back, maybe I had expedited my death-date by mentally crossing over. Somehow had given Death a chunk of the time I had left?*

No, no. Well, maybe. Thad wasn't sure. How could he be? *What do those who haven't died yet know about death, the voices had expressed to me. And, although I had mentally crossed over, I still know nothing about death.*

The casket felt comfortable. So comfortable, in fact, Thad might have to replace his bed with one. *I would like to make love in one*, he thought. A coffin in his bedroom. If anyone found out, they would label him a vampire for sure. Warnings would spread until the fear became too great and some brave souls would have no choice but to drive a wooden stake through his heart.

Warning, Thad thought. *A warning I had crossed*

over and gone too far. 'Dead is dead,' the voice had said. 'Death still walks with you. Your consciousness has walked ahead into the void.'

Yes. Yes. A warning I had gone too far. Not physically dead, but mentally. My conscious.

Thad felt like he had it all figured out. Lying in the coffin, just as he had laid on the embalming table, had brought it all back.

Those moans, Thad remembered. *Agony. Pain. As if hearing someone being burned alive. Then many voices. Oh, so many. All of them in severe hell with no escape. And this fire inflicted the worst it had on them, yet, never consumed them, for I had heard them. How could that be?*

Yes, how could that be, indeed? Impossible? About as impossible as me dying and coming back.

About as impossible as me understanding what the hell had happened to me on that embalming table.

Thad sat up in the coffin, looked around the showroom, and laid back down.

Is this how death is going to be? Thinking and trying to figure things out?

It appalled him because it reminded him too much of life. And, like most people, this drove him nuts. Uncertainty always bred more uncertainty and uncertainty was a land void of truth, for truth resided in the land of certainty, a territory hard to find, but must exist. All answers lie there. Everything unexplainable has explanations, don't they? Reasons as to how and why those things occurred in the first place?

Thad believed so. Absolutes were real. They lived in the land of certainty. And a few times, not many, he swore he had wandered into that country and seen, smelled, tasted, heard, and touched truth. It may have only been in part, but it was there. Real. If he only had more time with it, he might understand it fully—without wrath and doubting.

Oh, how Thad wished that the casket could somehow take him to the land of certainty or bring it closer. It seemed so far away.

Maybe that's what I'm longing for? Not death itself, but truth. The land of certainty. Perhaps that's where the voice had spoken from? Because what's truer than death? Maybe death and truth are one and the same?

Thad crossed his arms over his chest and closed his eyes. This wasn't in his bedroom, but inside the funeral home, where he would end up someday. Nor was he in his pajamas, lying in bed, but wearing the suit he was to be buried in and lying in a coffin—the exact model and color he had chosen.

'Your consciousness has walked ahead into the void,' Thad remembered the voice had said. *'...the void...the void...the void.'*

So, if uncertainty was a land void of truth, why did

119

my crossed-over conscious go into the void instead of into truth—the land of certainty?

Taxing as all of this was and way past his usual bedtime, at five minutes to midnight, Thad wondered, *Maybe truth doesn't exist,* and he fell asleep. He had forgotten to pull the sheet up over his head in his ritual by not closing the casket lid.

22

AT the stroke of midnight, *"THADEUS!"* boomed inside the casket. Startled awake, Thad opened his eyes—and saw the casket was closed.

"THADEUS!" reverberated inside the corpse-container.

The voice sounded male to Thad. Strong.

Commanding. How God might sound, as depicted in most media.

A woman's voice this time. *"THADEUS!"* Mature. Wise. Piercingly-pitched to shatter the casket, like glass.

Thad shrieked at the sound of his name.

Then silence. Thad tried to speak, but only choking scratches came out. He *was* choking.

When he tried bringing his hands up to his throat, they wouldn't move—just as they wouldn't on the embalming table.

The woman cackled at this, enjoying his captivity.

The choking continued, then Thad realized it wasn't from anything he had instigated. No, he was being choked. By what, he didn't know, couldn't see or touch to know. No one can see their own neck except on a reflective surface.

All he could see was the coffin lid closed above him. No longer wondering how it closed, for he knew. What had him had closed it. And he could *feel* what had him. Hands, or things similar, so hot, they burned the skin around his neck. Whoever or whatever had him possessed unusual strength. And possibly invisible, for there was no sign of any movement.

Breathing became increasingly difficult with each passing second. The more Thad tried to move his hands, it became apparent that this wasn't the rigamortis he had experienced on the body-table in the embalming room. No, someone or something was restraining him, feeling that same heat around his wrists.

As soon as he tried moving his legs, a warm grip grabbed his ankles and held them down.

"*THADEUS!*" A male voice, possibly different than the first. Thad wasn't sure.

A bellowing laugh taunted Thad in not being able to move or speak. The laughter echoed inside the coffin as it might inside a large belly.

Heat passed through Thad's pantlegs to his ankles. Not as hot as on his neck and wrists, which sizzled from being cooked, but still, uncomfortably warm.

A euphoric state among lightheadedness brought on a high that contented Thad in blissful ignorance to the fact that life was being choked out of him. *Death* must be nearby, collecting his life-time at an expedited rate.

Experiencing a high he never had before, Thad swore he caught a glimpse of *Death* inside the casket with him. It wasn't anything like he would have guessed it to be. Throw out all previous depictions for they were wrong. An aurora Death was, similar to the Northern Lights, yet darker, but too active to be a shadow. For shadows don't sway and swirl in mid-air as this did inside the casket.

Nor did Thad feel those burns around his neck, wrists, and ankles any longer, despite layers of skin missing; the bottoms of his pantlegs no longer there.

Good thing Thad couldn't see how bad the burns were. If he could, he wouldn't like what he would see. Flesh seared black and sunken below surrounding healthy tissue and—more pronounced around the neck—in the shape of an opened hand with clearly defined fingers under an overlapping hand.

"Is this what you want, Thad?" the voices, male and female, asked collectively.

How in the world Thad was supposed to answer, he didn't know or care. His mind was slipping. Any obligation to respond didn't register.

Who are you? Thad thought, more interested in knowing who his killers were than answering their question.

"Not much time, Thad. What'll it be? Life or death?"

Although Thad's state of mind was dreamy and carefree, the question registered. To him, it didn't seem unethical, immoral, or offensive. It was just a question. And his state of consciousness made it easy to answer, for he found it agreeable.

Death, Thad answered in thought.

23

THE thought had been enough for the voices to carry out the act. Thad laid there and accepted it. Never in his life had he ever felt so carefree. So, detached from the world. A world that didn't seem to hold the truth. All of it a lie. A system manipulated by a few to oppress the majority. Wealth. Possessions. Opportunity.

And once established early in human existence, little had changed since.

Thad felt that way because he was leaving this world. And everything behind. His assets. Apartment. And that crummy part-time gig babysitting animals like Muncie, the cat.

So fucking what? It wasn't much. Nothing really. A farting sphincter zero when compared to trillionaires, billionaires, and millionaires. No, he would die with a lot less. When a person's everything amounts to nothing, what was there to keep him around? Nothing gained, so nothing to lose.

But it wasn't all bad. There were a few people he would miss. Mr. Still. Alice. Gretchen. Costa, not so much. Only a few around town he could count on one hand. All acquaintances, though.

Then there was everybody else. Those Thad wouldn't miss at all. Mrs. Dray. All of the other animal owners in the apartment building. Especially those who never came to him for his services. Those bleeding assholes.

Usually, those who long to leave this world have been dealt a shitty hand. A non-winner. And the advice to play the hand dealt you just doesn't cut the mustard when the cards aren't sharp enough to cut your own wrist, let alone slice through all of the bullshit to rise to the top where all of the means, meaning, and magic happens.

That was Thad in a nutshell. Not much would change in his life between now and a future-death-date, and he knew it. Too many things would have to line up for a significant change to come. And the odds of that happening were slim to none. Statistics could be manipulated to communicate anything, but overall, trends don't lie.

So why prolong the agony? The pain? Especially when Thad felt pretty good about now. There were worse ways of dying than being choked to death. And this fit the bill to be surely talked about and remembered as one of those strange, unusual, unexplainable, and mysterious deaths.

Man wearing suit found dead in coffin inside funeral home

It ends right, Thad thought.

Departure felt right and better than expected. Kind of like going to sleep without all of the stressors to keep him awake.

Without fighting it, Thad laid in the coffin and dreamed. Crazier stuff than when he dreamed alive. Less oxygen reaching the brain will conjure far-out dreams like that.

In-and-out Thad went. Numerous times, occupying his mind and body one moment, to peeking outside his corpse into the afterlife the next. Until he found the courage to abandon the familiar and proceed into the unknown.

Death had collected all there was to collect from Thadeus E. Hadet.

24

TO Thad's surprise, he woke up. Not woke up—woke up as alive on Earth, but awakened in another world. A world of dreams, there enough to make anyone believe it to be real, yet allusive enough anything was possible. Perhaps, a conscious state without the need for a physical body. Yet, in examining himself, his body felt real enough. It was the body-table inside the embalming room all over again.

Or so he thought. It was worse. Way worse. And there was nothing he could do about it.

What he saw could only be described as Hell. Forget about all of the overused clichés of the word, especially when used for a situation not that bad. This was bad. Evil. So much so that he longed to be someplace else—much in the same way he had longed on Earth.

But how does anyone escape death? Leave death? Thad didn't know, but he searched like hell for a way.

No longer in the casket or pinned by invisible hands, he wished he hadn't seen this. Wished he hadn't heard it. Wished he hadn't smelled it.

At first, it was hard for Thad to make out exactly what he saw because it was too far away. It was terrible, he knew. A blob of humanity perhaps, together on what looked like a mattress. How many and what they were doing, he couldn't tell.

Something not right about it: groans and moans of pain or pleasure, he couldn't tell which. And a godawful smell came from that direction. Body odor, Thad guessed, because he had never smelled B.O. that pungent, but it was familiar enough. Dirt. Sweat. Uncleanliness.

Mixed with something. Sour. Yeasty. Fecal.

He couldn't tell whether he was moving toward the eyesore or if it was moving toward him. Probably the latter, because there was no way he would have proceeded toward it. Not ever. Some things were better left alone. Avoid getting entangled in such matters seemed wise. Turn and go in the opposite direction.

For some reason, Thad couldn't. Couldn't even look away. He didn't have control of himself. And as the unsettling image and Thad moved toward one another, details of what he saw sharpened. Gradually, the sight of the unspeakable worsened. And as he started distinguishing those details, that's when it became unbearable.

There were people, alright—two of them, laying on top of one another. Their arms appeared to be blended. Attached. Both having and sharing the same set of arms. Based on their haircuts, two men—yes, definitely men. Moaning and groaning as they appeared to be grinding hips against one another. Both were facing down toward the mattress. Homosexuals. Their bodies emitted the worst odor Thad had ever smelled. As if these two grown men had never showered a day in their life—or death—if that's what this was. Or brushed their teeth. Or wiped their ass after taking a shit.

Their faces weren't visible. Then the one on top turned and looked right at Thad, licking his lips.

Now there's a sight Thad wished he had never seen. Women were Thad's thing, not men. But there he was, intruding. Uncomfortable—definitely.

Where's Death, Thad thought. *The Collector. Because I want a refund. Enough to get back, re-die, and see if I'm lucky enough to end up someplace else.*

Then, Thad recognized the face. Oh, how he wished he hadn't. It was Gus Gainell, who had died last week in his sleep.

I never knew he was gay? Thad thought, then, *Why would I?*

"Thad," Gus said after a pleasurable moan. "Come join us."

"Not my thing, Gus," Thad said flatly.

"Suit yourself."

Then, the other man turned toward Thad; his face covered in sweat and he appeared out of breath.

"I'll be damned," the man said. "Thad Hadet."

Unfortunately, Thad recognized him, too. "Mr. Lockie?"

"Ooh," Mr. Lockie said, arching his neck back. "That's good." Then, he snapped his face

toward Thad again and said, "Looks like you're damned, too. I knew you weren't a God-man, but I'd never thought I'd see you here. Especially so soon."

Coffin-bangers, Thad thought. *Gainell and Lockie. Maybe in real life, too. If they were, they hid it well.*

"That makes two of us on both accounts," Thad said.

Startling Thad, a third head appeared out from between the two men. A woman.

"Ms. Peachtree?"

Thad had been wrong. There weren't two people, but three. Yet, sharing the same set of arms attached to each of their bodies at the shoulder sockets, connecting the three of them like the wheels on a train.

They were training it, alright, Thad thought. *But not like any train I have ever seen.*

Closer now, what Thad could see was that the arm was something less than an arm in not having elbows or hands. Straight this was. Solid bone covered with flesh and skin, running from Gainell's shoulders to Peachtree's and attached to Lockie's, a single rod attached to three pistons.

Ms. Peachtree yelled in pleasure and pain, then looked at Thad. "Young Thadeus. You want in on this, you young, depraved stud?"

Everything about it made Thad gag. These coffin-bangers were training it to a destination he didn't want to go—a place he shouldn't be.

All three of them were facing down: Mr. Gainell into Ms. Peachtree's backdoor and Missus into Mr. Lockie. Their aged bodies were flabby—and dead. Pale. Dry. Flaky. Shrunken.

Thad had been shown too much. Hopefully, he would be spared the details of Ms. Peachtree and Mr. Lockie's connection.

"You've got plenty going on there already, Ms. Peachtree," Thad said.

This was no time for a snicker.

"Says you," the old woman said.

Closer, now, Thad got a better view of the mattress. Everything hitting his senses overpowered them. His eyes watered, begging for blindness. His nose dripped, wanting to lose its ability. His ears rang, desiring deafness. His mouth was dry—and that was just fine. And when he gagged, he failed to vomit, only dry-heaved.

Just when he thought nothing could gross him out more than three old coffin-bangers banging one another, attached to each other by two, irregular arms, of course, in Hell, something topped it. For the mattress the departed geezers fucked on wasn't a mattress at all. It was the Elutes' bloated bodies. Pale with the same gashes, gouges, and gaps in the flesh, only they were now white-washed. And entirely naked; the strips of clothing that remained when the bodies were found were now gone.

When Thad looked down to avert his eyes, Mr. Gainell was under him. Ms. Peachtree under Gainell. And Mr. Lockie under her. Thad was naked. Gainell's body felt oily against his skin, like the juice inside a can of tuna fish, which surprised Thad, how dry Gainell looked.

Thad's mouth gaped, sounds came out. Not of pleasure, certainly pain, but mostly horror. He should have known something was up when he was invited to join in.

Yes, the horror only Hell can twist and conjure.

When Thad went to move off Gainell, he realized his hands were gone and his arms were now part of the rod-arms of the coffin-bangers, which were now attached at his shoulders.

Thad closed his eyes and begged, "Please stop!"

Feeling something on top of him, Thad opened his eyes. Now, he found himself sandwiched between the Elute's bloated bodies. Dead, they were supposed to be. But they were moving, in particular, grinding—on Thad— emitting sounds of pleasure.

Something wiggled on Thad's butt. Thad

tried not thinking about it, because Mrs. Elute was on top of him.

Quite the contortionist Hell was, twisting all it could into the unseemingly.

"Please stop!" Thad cried. *"Please!* Make it stop!"

His arms were melding with the Elutes' to create that entrapping rod with them. He closed his eyes and screamed, "I didn't want to die to this! Take me back! *Take me back!"*

25

NO longer feeling the Elutes' bloated bodies against him, Thad opened his eyes. Above him, the casket cover. More welcoming than where he had just come from, but not as much as when he had first laid down. The peace he used to associate immediately with caskets had been robbed from him. So much so, he would never look at caskets the same way again.

When he tried opening the lid, it wouldn't.

Thad laid there, crying. Although he was fully dressed in the suit he was to be buried in, he could still feel the oil on his body and smell that odor, lingering on.

Yes, Hell. No doubt, Thad had been there. Who or what else could have come up with such a horrible nightmare? Only Hell and its Hellions, that's who.

"Told you, you were taking this too far," a man's voice said in the usual, human communicating way.

Thad recognized it now.

"Gainell?" Thad asked, but he was pretty sure.

"That's my name," Gainell said. "Don't wear it out."

"Tell me that didn't happen."

"You bet my ass it did!"

"Oh, man. Not the answer I wanted."

"Relax," Gainell said. "You weren't really part of it. Not physically, anyway."

"Oh, thank God! Or Sat…"

"Don't say it, Thad! *Do not* say that name. You remember what happened last time?"

"Or, whoever deserves the credit," Thad settled on.

"Whew!" Gainell said, a little out of breath. "I

thought for sure you were gonna say it."

"*Na.* You cut me a break, so I thought I'd return the favor. But I still might if you actually did those things."

"Now Thad, that's my business, not yours. You have other business to attend to. And remembering what you saw is part of it."

"Then, I don't want any part of it," Thad said, flatly.

"You better remember it!" Gainell warned. "Because if you don't, you'll be back here repeating what you witnessed."

"*Why?* I don't deserve that."

"And I do?" Gainell asked, wondering.

"Sorry," Thad said.

"No, what's sorry is how far you took this, Thad. Sure, everyone knows this whole thing ends in death, no matter how or when. But, for fuck's sake, don't waste living years with dead ones."

"You had to say it that way, didn't you?"

"Why sure. In fact, every time you have sex, you'll remember what you saw. The very act will trigger that memory."

"You just ruined my life."

"It's not like it's going to happen very often."

"*Gee,* thanks," Thad said. "I take it, you know?"

"Can't say," Gainell said. "All I know is your *longing* is going to cross you over *prematurely* and *permanently* one of these days, and then you'll be spending eternity with us."

"You, Peachtree, and Lockie?"

"And the Elutes."

"I don't want that."

"You're a sexy bitch, Thad E. Hadet, but we don't either. Not yet, anyway."

"So, now what?" Thad asked. "What do I do?"

"Live," Gainell said. "And don't come back here until it's your turn to be here."

"When will that be?"

Not hearing anything, Thad asked again, "When will that be, Gainell?—Gainell?"

Thad pressed on the coffin lid—and it opened.

26

LATE morning, inside the Will. B. Still Funeral Home, Costa and Mr. Still crossed paths in the hallway.

"Hey, you happen to straighten out Thad's casket change?" Mr. Still asked.

"I started running some numbers," Costa started, "but I'm not sure how much we can take off of that particular model if I have the right one from the note he left…"

"*Note?*"

"Yeah," Costa pointed toward his office. "On my desk."

"When *exactly* did Thad leave it?"

"Well, I don't know. Had to be yesterday sometime."

"*Wait a minute!* You haven't seen him today?"

"No, not yet."

"What about Alice?"

"Don't know. I haven't stopped to talk…"

"*Mm.* Gretchen?"

"Gretchen doesn't come in…"

Waving a hand, Mr. Still said, "Not until later, I know."

Mr. Still covered his mouth with his hand, thinking.

"Strange bird, that guy," Costa said. "I mean, you ever look closely at his name?"

"*Huh?—Oh, uh*—no," Mr. Still rejoined the discussion. "No, I haven't."

"Well, I have. Both ways. Like playing a record forward and backward. And you want to know what I found. Thad E. Hadet, as in Thad *had it—h—a—d*, space, *i—t.* You get it?"

"Yeah, yeah. Like fed up."

"Exactly. And when you flip the record over, it gets weirder. If you take his first name, *Thad,* and his middle initial, *E*, and arrange the letters, you get *death*. Same goes for his last name without having to use his middle initial because all of the letters are already there. Isn't that strange? *Death-death* for a name."

"That *is* strange. What about his middle name, not initial?"

"Why, I've never thought about it. All we might have is his initial."

"Get on that, will you? *Oh*, and another thing, make sure his file is updated with all of his requests, including that Spanish-Gray casket with the white interior. And Costa—take the $500 off."

"Are you sure? We might have to eat…"

"*Just* … do it, before I change my mind."

"Okay," Costa said. "And, oh, the rear passenger tire on the hearse needs air."

Impressed, Mr. Still's face lit up when he asked. "Is that so? You checked them this morning?"

"No. Thad mentioned it in his letter."

Disappointment in Costa deflated the hopeful expression on Mr. Still's face. "What is he, *a mechanic?* I guess he noticed it on his tour yesterday."

Costa shrugged. "I guess so."

Mr. Still shook his head. "Strange. You know that man's been coming here every day since he

143

was twelve-years-old. I mean *every day*. Except for closings, holidays, those types of things. Hell, he's got a better attendance record than you do and *you* work here."

"Twelve?" Costa said. "Why so long?"

Mr. Still put a hand on Costa's shoulder and said, "How about one of these slow days, I'll tell you over lunch?"

"If you're buying?"

"It's on me."

"Okay, then."

Mr. Still patted Costa's shoulder once and squeezed. "Okay."

He watched Costa walk back to his office, his mind on Thad.

I guess when someone's been longing for death as long as Thad has, there comes a time when either the longing fulfills itself or it stops.

In this business, Mr. Still had had his own bouts with longing for death. And if this business had taught him anything, it's once you're dead, you're dead. There are no start-overs or re-dos. At least being alive, he could stop something in his life and start again. It may not be fun or pretty, in fact, it might be downright ugly and nasty, but it could be done—where death can not.

He shook his head, smiled, and said, "End of an era."

As he walked back to his office, the smile waned. He felt empty, lonely.

I'm going to miss that pudding-puller around here. I truly am.

Oh, Mr. Still would see Thad around town, but it wouldn't be the same. Which was good for Thad, he knew. And he would always have to remember that.

At least the corpses can relax a little, he jokingly thought. *Thad made them nervous whenever he was around.*

Mr. Still entered his office, pulled open a drawer, and retrieved a key. Heading back down the hall, he whistled, spinning the key ring around his finger, planning on taking the hearse to get air in the tires and stop at Thad's place to make sure he was okay.

Passing Costa's office, he thought of something, backtracked, peeked his head in, and said, "One more thing, Costa, before I forget. Please pull yesterday's and last night's surveillance tapes."

"Sure," Costa said. "Which one would you like to see first?"

"Two, actually. The embalming room and showroom."

"Okay."

"And Costa."

"Yeah."

"You haven't told Gretchen about the hidden cameras we just put in, have you?"

"No. I figured she saw them cleaning. Why?"

"*Hmm*. No reason. Well, good. Don't."

ABOUT **THE AUTHOR**

W. G. TUTTLE is an American writer of riveting science fiction, thriller, and suspense novels and short stories. He is the author of the novels Try To Sleep, Those Who Long, October Midnight, and War For The Spheres. He has also written numerous short stories, including Scranton October 1894, Vacation's End, Where Did THEY Come From?, and Standard Issue Spirits.

He also writes screenplays and intelligent non-fiction about stocks, investing, and trading.

Born: January 27, 1972, Binghamton, New York

Full name: Walter George Tuttle, Jr.

Spouse: Shawn M. Tuttle (m.1997)

Children: 1 son & 1 daughter

Alma mater: The Pennsylvania State University

Influenced by: Frank Herbert, H. G. Wells, Ramsey Campbell (Carl Dreadstone), Arthur C. Clarke, Isaac Asimov, Stanislaw Lem, William Peter Blatty, Ira Levin, Robert Bloch, Ian Fleming, Alistair MacLean

wgtuttle.com

www.ingramcontent.com/pod-product-compliance
Lightning Source LLC
Chambersburg PA
CBHW051922240626
47153CB00004B/1328